TSCHANDALA

August Strindberg

AUGUST STRINDBERG (1849-1912) is best known outside Sweden as a dramatist, but he was also a prolific writer of novels, short stories, essays, journalism and poetry – as well as a notable artist and photographer. Although Strindberg was born and raised in Stockholm, and died there in 1912, he spent many years living abroad, in Switzerland, France, Germany, Austria and Denmark. It was his stay in Denmark in the 1880s which forms the background to *Tschandala*: in April 1888, together with his wife Siri and their three children, Strindberg took lodgings at the manor house of Skovlyst near Copenhagen. The visit was a disaster: he fell out with the estate factor, feeling himself suspected, amongst other things, of the theft of the estate's peacocks, and he had a short-lived affair with the factor's sister before fleeing the estate. *Tschandala* gives Strindberg's side of the business, presented in the guise of a historical setting.

PETER GRAVES lectures in Swedish at the University of Edinburgh, where he is the Head of the School of Literatures, Languages and Cultures. His particular research interests are translation and reception studies, and among his earlier published translations are Carl Linné's *Lapland Journey* and Jacob Wallenberg's *My Son on the Galley*. He is currently working on a new translation of Strindberg's *Röda rummet* (The Red Room), to be published by Norvik Press.

Some other books from Norvik Press

Victoria Benedictsson: *Money* (translated by Sarah Death)
Hjalmar Bergman: *Memoirs of a Dead Man* (translated by Neil Smith)
Jens Bjørneboe: *Moment of Freedom* (translated by Esther Greenleaf Mürer)
Jens Bjørneboe: *Powderhouse* (translated by Esther Greenleaf Mürer)
Jens Bjørneboe: *The Silence* (translated by Esther Greenleaf Mürer)
Johan Borgen: *The Scapegoat* (translated by Elizabeth Rokkan)
Fredrika Bremer: *The Colonel's Family* (translated by Sarah Death)
Suzanne Brøgger: *A Fighting Pig's Too Tough to Eat* (translated by Marina Allemano)
Camilla Collett: *The District Governor's Daughters* (translated by Kirsten Seaver)
Kerstin Ekman: *Witches' Rings* (translated by Linda Schenck)
Kerstin Ekman: *The Spring* (translated by Linda Schenck)
Kerstin Ekman: *The Angel House* (translated by Sarah Death)
Kerstin Ekman: *City of Light* (translated by Linda Schenck)
Janet Garton (ed.): *Contemporary Norwegian Women's Writing*
Knut Hamsun: *Selected Letters* (2 vols.) (edited and translated by James McFarlane and Harald Næss)
P. C. Jersild: *A Living Soul* (translated by Rika Lesser)
Viivi Luik: *The Beauty of History* (translated by Hildi Hawkins)
Runar Schildt: *The Meat-Grinder and Other Stories* (translated by Anna-Liisa & Martin Murrell)
Amalie Skram: *Lucie* (translated by Katherine Hanson & Judith Messick)
Amalie and Erik Skram: *Caught in the Enchanter's Net: Selected Letters* (edited and translated by Janet Garton)
Hjalmar Söderberg: *Martin Birck's Youth* (translated by Tom Ellett)
Hjalmar Söderberg: *Selected Stories* (translated by Carl Lofmark)
Edith Södergran: *The Poet Who Created Herself: Selected Letters* (edited and translated by Silvester Mazzarella)
Hanne Marie Svendsen: *Under the Sun* (translated by Marina Allemano)
Helene Uri: *Honey Tongues* (translated by Kari Dickson)
Elin Wägner: *Penwoman* (translated by Sarah Death) (2008)

TSCHANDALA

A Novella

by

August Strindberg

Translated from the Swedish and
with an Introduction by

Peter Graves

Originally published in Danish translation under the title
Tschandala (1889), and in Swedish in 1897.

This translation and introduction © Peter Graves 2007.

The Translator has asserted his moral right to be identified as the
Translator of the work in relation to all such rights as are granted by
the Translator to the Publisher under the terms and conditions of their
contract.

*A catalogue record for this book is available from the British
Library.*
ISBN 978-1-870041-71-3
First published in 2007 by Norvik Press, University of East Anglia,
Norwich NR4 7TJ.

Norvik Press gratefully acknowledges the financial assistance given
by the University of Edinburgh towards the publication of this book.

Norvik Press was established in 1984 with financial support from the
University of East Anglia, the Danish Ministry for Cultural Affairs, the
Norwegian Cultural Department and the Swedish Institute.

e-mail address: norvik.press@uea.ac.uk
website: www.norvikpress.com

Managing editors: Janet Garton, Neil Smith, C. Claire Thomson.

Cover illustration: *Allén* (*The Avenue*, 1905) by August Strindberg.
Thielska Galleriet, Stockholm.

Cover design: Richard Johnson

Printed in the UK by Page Bros. (Norwich) Ltd, Norwich, UK

Contents

* * *

Tschandala:
Prejudice and the Spirit of the Age

August Strindberg is best known internationally as Sweden's greatest dramatist. Less well known outside Sweden is the range of his other creative work – novels, short stories, essays, journalism, poetry, and his paintings, which in recent decades have received the critical attention they merit. His ability to spark controversy on the issues of the day was enormous, as was his productivity: the National Edition of his collected works now approaching completion will run to seventy-two volumes; the publication of his collected letters fills twenty-two volumes. Born in Stockholm in 1849 into a well-off bourgeois family, he frequently preferred, as in the title of his autobiographical novel *Tjänstekvinnans son* (Son of a Serving Woman, 1886), to stress the less elevated social origins of his mother. After trying his hand first as a medical student and then as an apprentice actor at the Royal Dramatic Theatre he became a student of Aesthetics at the University of Uppsala in 1867. He left the university in 1872 without completing his studies, which is less than surprising given that he had written no fewer than six plays in that time, including his first major drama *Mäster Olof* (Master Olof, 1872), a historical drama set at the time of the Swedish Reformation in the early sixteenth century. Returning to Stockholm, he earned his living as a freelance writer, journalist and later librarian, living in the poorer quarters of the city in a bohemian milieu of artists and writers. These years provided the material for his breakthrough novel *Röda rummet* (The Red Room, 1879), a satire of contemporary society. The novel was a public success, caused a furore, and also marked a new level of literary realism in Swedish writing.

In 1877 he had married the Finland-Swedish aristocrat Siri von Essen after a courtship that involved taking her from her first husband. The couple and their three children spent the greater part of the 1880s outside Sweden in France, Switzerland, Germany and latterly Denmark, and it was during this period of exile that the great trio of naturalistic dramas – *Fadren* (The Father, 1887), *Fröken Julie* (Miss Julie, 1888) and *Fordringsägare* (Creditors, 1888) – were written. The struggle for power between the sexes, at least partly a reflection of his own marital turmoil, lies at the heart of these plays – and they gained him his lasting reputation as a misogynist. But during the same period he wrote, often reluctantly and in haste since they took him away from the serious work of drama, the novels and short stories necessary to financial survival. Those works set in the islands of the Stockholm archipelago in particular – *Hemsöborna* (The People of Hemso, 1887), *Skärkarlsliv* (Life in the Skerries, 1888) and *I havsbandet* (By the Open Sea, 1890) – won public popularity, not least because of their lighter tone and the author's manifest affection for that region.

On his return to Sweden in 1889 he settled in the archipelago but following the bitter break-up of his marriage with Siri von Essen he moved abroad again in 1892, first to Berlin, thereafter to Austria during his second marriage with the Austrian journalist Frida Uhl, and finally Paris. These years of renewed exile are marked by financial penury, spiritual crisis and the psychological breakdown that led to his desertion of literature for the pseudo-sciences of alchemy and occultism. He describes the period in the autobiographical novel *Inferno* (1897) which marks his return to literature and introduces the period of the great and formally pioneering dramas of spiritual search, conversion and, intermittently, reconciliation: *Till Damaskus I-II* (To Damascus, 1898), *Advent* (1898) and *Ett drömspel* (A Dream Play, 1901). He returned to Stockholm in 1899 and remained there, still writing prolifically in both prose and dramatic forms until his death in 1912.

Tschandala, the novella translated into English here for the first time (it has been translated into Danish, French, German and Italian), was written in the autumn of 1888, the year that also saw the creation of such better known dramatic works as *Miss Julie* and *Creditors* as well as the stories in the volume *Life in the Skerries*. The publication history of *Tschandala* is complex. It was intended to be one of the stories in a series of historical tales (or rather, tales in historical dress) *Svenska öden och äventyr* (Swedish Destinies and Adventures, 1883-91) which Strindberg produced as a jobbing writer, one might say, between works he considered of more importance throughout the 1880s. It was rejected by Claës Looström, publisher of the series, and then also rejected by Karl-Otto Bonnier to whom Strindberg had sent it next: Bonnier demanded changes that Strindberg was not prepared to make. So it was first published in a Danish translation by Peter Nansen in 1889 and did not appear in Swedish until 1897, by which stage Strindberg's original manuscript had gone astray and what was published was a Swedish back-translation by Eugene Fahlstedt. The National Edition has a new translation from the Danish by Torbjörn Nilsson.

As with so much that Strindberg wrote, *Tschandala* has an autobiographical background – in this case a background as strange as the story it inspired. In 1887 he moved to Denmark and at the end of April 1888, together with his wife Siri and their three children, he took lodgings at the manor house of Skovlyst near Copenhagen.[1] His marriage was in trouble though it was to be another four years before it was finally dissolved. The owner of Skovlyst was Countess Louise de Frankenau, then aged forty, and her estate factor was the twenty-six year-old Ludvig Hansen, her illegitimate half-brother though, according to local rumour, her lover. The countess was an animal lover and her estate was an unofficial sanctuary for them: in Strindberg's account the animals are neglected and mistreated but Louise de Frankenau's successor at Skovlyst testifies that they were in fact well cared for. The factor, Ludvig Hansen, was an unstable character: a carpenter by trade but an amateur actor, writer and conjurer with no experience of running a farm or estate, which was thus in serious decline and financial difficulty. He was unpopular in the district and something of a figure of scorn. Nevertheless, it seems that he and Strindberg started off on very good terms but became estranged when Strindberg felt himself suspected of the theft of the estate's peacocks. The estrangement deepened during August, possibly as a result of Strindberg's short affair with Hansen's seventeen-year old sister Martha Magdalene, and by the end of the month Hansen was attempting to drive out the Strindberg family even though the rent had been paid until the end of September. The family left Skovlyst in haste on 2 September after a violent scene between Strindberg and Hansen during which the latter seems to have told Siri of her husband's affair with Martha Magdalene. In an anonymous letter to the legal advice column of the newspaper *Politiken*, seeking advice on how to reclaim his rent for September, Strindberg describes the run-up to his departure in the following words:

> my landlord sets his dogs on me, allows the house to be fouled by latrines, gets drunk, screams and shouts the whole night, breaks into my rooms in a drunken state, abuses my family when they are sitting eating their meal, fires off a revolver at three o'clock in the morning outside my windows, dances like a Red Indian outside my door at the same time as making a horrendous racket with sheets of zinc – all this with the clear intention of forcing me to move before the end of my tenancy...[2]

Leaving Skovlyst was not, however, to be the end of the episode. Strindberg now denounced Hansen to the police as the possible perpetrator of a series of thefts in the district and Hansen seems to have leaked the affair with Martha Magdalene to the press, where it variously figured as under-age sex or even rape. Strindberg considered legal action but had to be satisfied with a statement of denial published in *Politiken*:

With regard to the shameful rumours spread about me by my literary enemies, I would hereby like to inform my friends and kinsmen that I have not raped children, nor have I been involved in the burglaries in Taarbaek.[3]

Only two days after his hasty departure from Skovlyst Strindberg was writing to Edvard Brandes with thoughts of a story based on the summer's experiences:

Since 1 May I have been spending the summer at a most extraordinary place in the country, from where I have been hounded by revolver shots, break-ins, gypsy dances and eight dogs, after having paid the rent for September in advance. I am now installed at the Hotel Nyholte, mourning my lost money, my honour, and my books, which the wretch has seized against some false bills. This will be a novel shortly![4]

The 'shortly' was, in fact, immediate and the novella was complete by the middle of December. Strindberg has given the novella an historical rather than a contemporary setting, something he felt tactically necessary even though he considered that it weakened the story. The time is the 1690s and, rather than Denmark, the location is Skåne, the southern province that Sweden annexed from Denmark in 1658 and retained after the war of 1675-79. The protagonist, Master Andreas Törner, is a Swedish academic at the University of Lund, charged among other things with the Swedicisation of a recalcitrant Danish student population. His superiors command him to remain in the province during his summer vacation in order to sound out local feelings and attitudes, so he and his family rent rooms in the dilapidated manor house Bögely, where his hosts are an eccentric baroness and her factor Jensen, a gipsy. There Törner, although puzzled by the peculiarities of the people and environment, initially enjoys a good relationship with the people of the house and attempts to provide guidance on the running of the estate, but he is drawn into conflict with the factor/gipsy whom he suspects of lies, intrigues and criminality as well as incompetence. The conflict intensifies after Törner's sexual encounter with the gipsy's sister and culminates in a drawn-out struggle for survival between the two men, which Törner wins in a macabre denouement by playing on the gipsy's credulity and superstition. The atmosphere and setting of the story are thoroughly Gothic: the ruinous castle, mystery and suspense, inexplicable events, strange aristocrats and gipsies, baying hounds, unexplained howls and eerie sounds. For Strindberg himself, however, who had not read Edgar Allan Poe until shortly after completing *Tschandala*, it was Poe who came to mind; writing to Ola Hansson in January 1889 he speculates on whether he (born in the same year as Poe died) could be a reincarnation of Poe's spirit and comments:

> On the night between Christmas Day and Boxing Day I read Edgar Poe for the first time! And noted it in my diary! I'm astounded! Is is possible that he † in 49, the year I was born, and could have smouldered down through hosts of spirits to me! What are 'The Battle of the Brains', 'Short Cuts', *The Secret of the Guild* even (I read the Danish proofs of this today), other than E.P![5]

And a month later: 'At the moment I'm proof reading the Danish edition of *Tschandala*. It's Poe before Poe! Absolutely!'[6]

On one level, as Martin Lamm pointed out, the novella is Strindberg's paranoid settling-of-scores with Ludvig Hansen after the summer at Skovlyst. Its interest, Lamm says, lies in it being a 'psychological document' and it is a prelude to his more profound mental crisis during the Inferno period of the 1890s.[7] Even allowing for that and recognising the raw, undigested nature of the autobiographical material, it has to be said that the image it presents of its creator is a profoundly unattractive one, an impression that is reinforced if Strindberg's correspondence of the period is read alongside the text. *Tschandala*, to use the terminology of today, is racist, sexist and class-conscious, all of which may account for some tendency to marginalise it as a literary text, to suggest without great justification – as Lamm did – that it is one of Strindberg's weaker texts, and to provide a partial explanation of why it has not appeared in English earlier.

Certainly, contemporary reviewers were, with few exceptions, negative in their reception of the novella. Most found it unconvincing in its characterisation, motivation and resolution and they were suspicious of and unsympathetic to the Nietzschean ideas it propounds, which are variously described as 'disgusting' and 'repulsive'.[8] The modern reader will undoubtedly share the moral discomfort implicit or explicit in the comments of the early reviewers, but for all its prejudice and unpleasantness *Tschandala* remains a fascinating and revealing work: there are few texts in which the personal and intellectual sources of the narrative lie closer to the surface, and there are few texts that reveal the darker aspects of the *Zeitgeist* more nakedly. Evert Sprinchorn in his elegant and persuasive essay 'Strindberg and the Superman' argues that any reading of Strindberg's work from the years around 1890 simply as a case history of a disturbed man is a misreading, and the 'true significance [of the works] lies in the fact that they record the tremors of a whole civilisation about to collapse'.[9] *Tschandala*, while being 'one of the most distasteful stories that Strindberg ever wrote', is 'based on that historical development'.[10]

The source of the conflict in the novella between Törner and Jensen is not a specific event, rather a set of feelings, attitudes and suspicions. The action, as in other of Strindberg's works of the period, represents a battle of wills, a power struggle between representations of human types as much as individuals: upper class versus lower; Aryan versus pariah; the intellectual versus the ignorant; the scientist versus the credulous; the honest versus the criminal; the moral versus the immoral; the liberal versus the lumpen – all subsumed in the characters of the scholar and the gipsy respectively. And the same struggle is simultaneously being waged within the mind of Törner since the 'noble', 'superior', 'moral' aspects of his being render him non-viable in the struggle for survival against an enemy who is elusive, mendacious and morally labile. Törner, it is stressed in the first half of the novella, is characterised by tolerance and an idealistic belief in the sanctity of the common people. He is happy to put his knowledge at the service of the gipsy and the estate and he is prepared to overlook Jensen's failures to fulfil his obligations and his habitual though usually petty mendacity, whatever his suspicions of lurking criminality may be. But as the months pass and it proves impossible for him to form any social relationships with the neighbours, partly because he is a Swede among conquered Danes and partly because he is perceived as a friend of the gipsy, Törner is restricted to the company of Jensen and finds himself increasingly influenced by him. He notes that he is taking on the gipsy's gestures and speech habits and he senses in himself an increasing nervousness, cowardice and uncertainty that are alien to him both as a scholar and as an old soldier. His decision is to leave Bögely as soon as possible and to put the whole business behind him. But that option is closed to him when his request for permission to leave is rejected in a message brought to him by his colleague Professor Bureus. Bureus is a man of very different metal: blunt, thuggish, a supporter of absolutism and rigid class distinctions, and his advice to Törner is to take a much more forceful and superior approach. Shortly after Bureus's visit Törner begins his fight back, but only after justifying himself by arguing that he is fighting the fight of the Greeks against the barbarians, that his survival is of greater value to mankind than that of the gipsy, that he is doing his duty by eradicating criminal elements, that the gipsy is a nomadic pariah of inferior race. To be certain of victory Törner must put aside his civilisation and culture, his honour and conscience, and murder like a barbarian in order to secure civilisation. And his final self-justification, after the killing of the gipsy, is couched in the words of the ancient Indian sage Manu, who defines the humiliations appropriate to the Tschandala, the lowest caste of humanity and the group in which Törner locates his adversary.

If, as Inga-Stina Ewbank has written, 'Strindberg's intellectual and spiritual development could be charted as a map of the ideological history of the second half of the nineteenth century: Kierkegaard, Darwin, Buckle, Spencer, Hegel, Nietzsche, Schopenhauer and so on...', *Tschandala* marks his enthusiastic discovery of Nietzsche during his time in Denmark.[11] In the spring of 1888 the Danish literary historian Georg Brandes gave a series of lectures in Copenhagen on the then virtually unknown Nietzsche, whom Brandes himself had only come across with the publication of Nietzsche's *Zur Genealogie der Moral* in 1887.[12] Nietzsche provided an alternative to the increasingly utilitarian and democratic positions taken by English philosophers and thanks to him Brandes had, in his own words, 'turned back ... to the Germans in philosophy'. Brandes now, like Nietzsche, 'favoured the morality of the few, the strong and solitary genius; arguing in favour of the "aristocracy of the mind" – or "*Herren-Moral*" – rather than accepting the dominance of the "uncivilised" masses'.[13] These lectures were fully reported in the Danish newspaper *Politiken* and it is here, immediately before his move to Skovlyst, that Strindberg first encountered the German philosopher. By the middle of May he is already writing to his younger contemporary Verner von Heidenstam: 'Buy a modern German philosopher called Nietzsche, about whom G.B. has been lecturing. Everything is there! Don't deny yourself this pleasure! N. is a poet too'.[14] And in September 1888 he writes in ecstatic terms to Edvard Brandes: 'However, the uterus of my mental mind has received a tremendous ejaculation of sperm from Friedrich Nietzsche, so that I feel like a bitch with a full belly. He's the man for me!'[15] In the period immediately before and during the writing of *Tschandala* Strindberg seems to have read *Jenseits von Gut und Böse*, *Der Fall Wagner*, *Götzendämmerung* and *Zur Genealogie der Moral*, as well as having a brief correspondence with Nietzsche – five letters from Nietzsche and four from Strindberg – in the autumn and early winter of 1888. Nietzsche's letters show all too clear signs of the madness that was to afflict him for the rest of his life and Strindberg, for the most part, writes in such ecstatically adulatory tones that his mental stability is also questionable:

15

Better to preserve your distinguished solitude and allow us ten thousand other elite spirits to make a secret pilgrimage to your sanctuary in order to imbibe at our pleasure. Let us protect your esoteric teaching by keeping it pure and inviolate, and not divulge it except through the medium of your devoted catechumens, among whom I sign myself.[16]

Nietzschean echoes are audible throughout *Tschandala*: the title itself and the novella's closing reference to the Laws of Manu occur in *Götzendämmerung*; the references to the Aryan springing from the warm dung of the underclass reflect ideas in *Jenseits von Gut und Böse*; the discussion of the master-slave morality reflect *Zur Genealogie der Moral*.[17] Michael Robinson has rightly pointed out that:

Strindberg's response to Nietzsche was unsystematic and partial; he assimilated only what fitted in with the aristocratic radicalism with which he was already experimenting. Thus, he was at least partly correct in maintaining (as he often did) that his initial enthusiasm reflected not a submission to Nietzsche's ideas, but a recognition of the ground they had in common, and even his most Nietzschean book, *By the Open Sea*, explores, rather than accepts, the limits of the position he currently adopted. In later years he severely criticised Nietzsche, either directly in *Gothic Rooms* or obliquely, as the madman Caesar, in *To Damascus*.[18]

In *Tschandala*, however, Strindberg's Nietzscheanism lacks all refinement of interpretation and differentiation – it is brute populist Nietzscheanism. The voice and behaviour of Bureus ('Rabble and dogs need thrashing! If you'd given that rogue a beating your time here would have been more pleasant!') becomes the dominant one. Although his presence in the narrative is short, his model and his advice lead Andreas Törner from the liberal democratic position he initially occupies to the aristocratic radical stance he finally espouses: the trajectory, however violently it may be depicted in *Tschandala*, effectively mirrors the philosophical shift Brandes saw as resulting from his own encounter with Nietzsche.

For his characterisation of the residents of Bögely Strindberg draws heavily on the theories of the Italian criminologist Cesare Lombroso (1836-1909). Lombroso, a biological determinist, argued that certain types of criminal – born criminals, that is those in whom the criminality is inherited – actually represent more primitive stages of human evolution. These types may be distinguished by atavistic physical stigmata. The gipsy, the baroness and Magellone all manifest some of the stigmata Lombroso considered typical of the atavistic criminal: peculiarities of the eyes (the gipsy, Magellone, the baroness); an abundance of wrinkles and lines (the gipsy); dental abnormalities (the baroness, Magellone, who also has a hint of vampirism); fleshy lips (the gipsy); unusual hair (the gipsy, Magellone). The non-physical characteristics of the Bögely residents also point to Lombroso: the excessive drinking, the compulsive lying, the suggestions of unfettered sexuality. Hans Lindström has noted, too, that Strindberg has almost certainly derived his motif of the inscriptions carved on the tree from Lombroso's discussion of criminal/savage hieroglyphics.[19]

Tschandala, then, depicts a conflict which in Nietzschean terms may be seen as being between the 'Übermensch' and its opposite, the 'tschandala' – it is both the gipsy and the 'tschandala' within, the slave mentality aspects of himself (Christian love, liberal values and so on), Törner must overcome in order to be victorious. In Lombroso's terms the conflict is between the born criminal type and the honourable man: for the honourable man to win he must resort to the methods of his criminal enemy. The extra element Strindberg adds, however, which in spite of general belief is absent in Nietzsche and also absent in Georg Brandes's writings on aristocratic radicalism, is that of race. In *Den Vita Handen och Den Svarta Handen* (The White Hand and The Black Hand), Strindberg's preliminary sketch for *Tschandala*, the racial origins of the two characters are not revealed; in the finished work the 'Übermensch', the Aryan, the honourable man is a Swede whereas the 'tschandala', the pariah, the born criminal is a gipsy – in other words,

17

Strindberg has opted to introduce race as a central factor in his exposition of the conflict. In focusing on the Roma as the enemies of Western civilisation Strindberg is, of course, using the shorthand of racial stereotyping and tapping in to the long tradition of anti-gipsy prejudice existing in all parts of Europe. The catalogue of negative traits ascribed to Jensen in *Tschandala* – rootlessness, indolence, lack of respect for landed property, superstition, mendacity, dishonesty, filth, sexuality, irrationality – can be found in popular belief and, indeed, in virtually all writings about the Roma: the romantic gipsy of Viktor Rydberg's novel *Singoalla* in Sweden or of George Borrow's books in Britain are exceptions.[20] The specific stimulus to Strindberg's choice of the gipsy as antagonist is again likely to have been Lombroso. In the latter part of the nineteenth century it is virtually impossible to separate speculation regarding the origins of criminality and criminals from Social Darwinist racial theorising. Lombroso, while searching for universal causes of criminality, frequently falls back on race as a determining factor: 'Race. This is of great importance in view of the atavistic origin of crime. There exist whole tribes and races more or less given to crime... In the gipsies we have an entire race of criminals with all the passions and vices common to delinquent types: idleness, ignorance, impetuous fury, vanity, love of orgies, and ferocity'.[21]

For many nineteenth-century thinkers the root of perceived gipsy criminality lay in the absence of what Carlyle called 'Permanence': 'Permanence, persistence is the first condition of all fruitfulness in the ways of men. The tendency to persevere, to persist in spite of hindrances, discouragements and impossibilities: it is this that in all things distinguishes the strong soul from the weak; the civilised burgher from the nomadic savage, – the Species man from the Genus Ape!'[22] Or as Andreas Törner expresses it in his ruminations in *Tschandala*: 'He and his kind are incapable of work. They cannot settle and found a nation or a family so they have been perpetual nomads, moving from country to country in search of loot and plunder'.

So *Tschandala*, on one level Strindberg's simple if vindictive settling-of-scores with the people of Skovlyst/Bögely in which the author's prejudices are nakedly revealed, proves to be a showcase of late nineteenth-century ideologies: Strindberg's prejudices are in the spirit of the age. We may find *Tschandala* morally reprehensible in its attitudes but what cannot be denied is that its author had an acute ear for the music of his time.

Notes

1. A full account of the Skovlyst period is given in Harry Jacobsen, *Digteren og fantasten: Strindberg paa Skovlyst*, Copenhagen, 1945.
2. Quoted from Gunnar Brandell, *Strindberg: Ett författarliv*, vol. 2, Stockholm, 1985, p.19.
3. Quoted from Harry Jacobsen, p.154.
4. Michael Robinson (ed.), *Strindberg's Letters Vol.1, 1862-1892*, London, 1992, p.282.
5. ibid., p.310.
6. ibid., p.305.
7. Martin Lamm, *August Strindberg*, Stockholm, 1948, p.218.
8. August Strindberg, *Samlade verk: Svenska öden och äventyr II*, (Nationalupplagan), ed. Bengt Landgren, 1990, pp.393-94.
9. Evert Sprinchorn, 'Strindberg and the Superman', in Göran Stockenström (ed.), *Strindberg's Dramaturgy*, Minneapolis, 1988, p.18.
10. ibid., p.19.
11. Inga-Stina Ewbank, 'August Strindberg', in Irene Scobbie (ed.), *Aspects of Modern Swedish Literature*, Norwich, 1999, p.37.
12. For a full account of Strindberg and Nietzsche see Harold Borland, *Nietzsche's Influence on Swedish Literature*, Gothenburg, 1956, pp.17-46.
13. Henk van der Liet, 'Georg Brandes as a Literary Intermediary', in *Tijdschrift voor Skandinavistiek*, 25.1, 2004, http://dpc.uba.uva.nl/tvs/vol25/nr01/art05
14. Michael Robinson, p.277.
15. ibid., p.283.

16. ibid., pp.294-95.
17. Harold Borland, pp.18-19.
18. Michael Robinson, p.294.
19. Hans Lindström, *Hjärnornas kamp. Psykologiska idéer och motiv i Strindbergs åttiotalsdiktning*, Uppsala, 1952, pp.199-200.
20. For discussion of Strindberg and gipsies see Sebastian Casinge, 'Zigenar- och tattarschabloner i August Strindbergs Tschandala', in *Strindbergiana*, no.16, Stockholm, 2002, pp.100-122.
21. Cesare Lombroso, *Criminal Man*, New York and London, 1911, pp.139-40. Lombroso's work first appeared in Italian as *L'uomo delinquente* in 1876; Strindberg was presumably familiar with the French translation *Homme criminel* of 1887. Given the marked anti-semitism of some of Strindberg's earlier writings and the intermittent expressions of anti-semitism throughout his life, it is perhaps surprising that he did not cast a Jew in the scapegoat role. This, too, is likely to be a result of his reading of Lombroso, who classifies Jews as among the least criminal races.
22. Thomas Carlyle, *Past and Present* (1843), ed. Richard D. Altick, New York, 1965, p.274.

Tschandala

Part I

One day in April towards the end of the reign of Karl XI Master
Andreas Törner, a learned lecturer at the University of Lund, was
sitting in his room in the half-timbered building on Lilla
Gråbrödragatan. His mood was melancholy. The students at the
recently established university, most of them Danes supposedly
learning the language and customs of Sweden, had been up to
their usual malicious practical jokes, raising a rumpus but doing it
so cleverly that it was impossible to apprehend the guilty ones.
Master Törner never approached the lectern without taking a
loaded horse-pistol from his back-pocket and ostentatiously
placing it alongside his glass of water, but today he had suffered
the indignity of ending up on the floor right at the beginning of his
lecture because someone had broken his chair and carefully glued
it back together very weakly. This – unfortunately – had not led to
an outburst of mirth so there was no-one he could blame and any
attempt to find the culprit would be about as useful as firing in the
air.

A further reason for dejection had emerged a little earlier since,
with the end of term approaching, Master Törner had reckoned on
being able to spend the summer in Växjö, his home town. But the
Principal had just informed him of a royal command that, in view
of the ferment in the conquered provinces, he must remain in this
part of the country and try to influence the minds of the obdurate;
and while conversing and socializing with the population he was
to acquaint himself with local attitudes. His task was to encourage
acceptance of the policy of integration into Sweden.

Being a university teacher in such times was no easy task and
in order to instil respect in the students the Principal only selected

strong and stout-hearted fellows who, when necessary, could take a firm grip on their audience. Master Andreas Törner had entered his academic career armed with a hawthorn cudgel with which he had beaten back an attack on the lectern for an hour and a half so vigorously that he and six students had to be admitted to the infirmary. He was a hard man, had been to the war in his youth, had taken part in the Battle of Lund back in 1676 and had a number of scars on his face. His subjects were politics and economics, the latter encompassing biology, botany, domestic economy and physics. With summer approaching and homesickness for the spruce-woods of his home province beginning to torment him – and with no prospect of being able to satisfy that longing – he was trying to find a house on the coast for the summer, hoping for an opportunity to collect plants and insects while living close to some decent woodland together with his wife and two children. Given the ill-will towards Sweden among the common people he had decided against taking lodgings with farmers or fishermen and was instead making enquiries among the tradesmen he patronized to see whether any of the gentry might be disposed to giving up a couple of rooms and a kitchen along with the necessary outhouses. He had just received a tip from a stallholder in the market about a likely place, the owner of which was expected in town any day.

Such summer thoughts, however, were not on his mind as he sat there in his leather chair smoking Dutch canaster. There was a knock at the door of his room. When he called 'Come in' in an absent-minded voice, the door was opened, at first only ajar and then wide-open, by a swarthy, fairly young man of medium height dressed like an affluent townsman. The man entered, casting quick glances round the room as if looking for something. He examined the desk and the bookcases before bowing humbly and smiling at Master Törner, who invited him to speak. But the man seemed disinclined to speak straight out. Instead, he twisted and turned and clearly wanted the lecturer to speak first in order to give him something to respond to.

'Who are you?' Törner inquired at last, both impatient and

unsettled.

'Please excuse me, Sir, but I've come about the summer accommodation,' the stranger replied, half in Danish, half in Swedish.

'Oh, I see,' said Törner in broken Danish to be accommodating. 'What do you have to offer?'

The unknown visitor seemed to be weighing up his answer, feeling his way in order to strike just the right note.

'I have a castle!' he finally blurted out.

Törner wrinkled his nose.

'That's to say, if that's what you want. May I ask what it is you are looking for, Sir?'

'I'm looking for a good residence with a garden.'

'Indeed! I'm a gardener,' the stranger interrupted him.

Master Törner thought his pale complexion was hardly that of a gardener but he let it pass.

'Are you the owner?' he continued.

'No, I'm not, I'm just the factor but the baroness herself is outside in her carriage if you wouldn't mind coming down, Sir.'

When Törner went downstairs he found the baroness – so-called, anyway – already involved in negotiations with his wife. She was sitting in a large carriage dating from the days of Queen Kristina, pulled by two Arab horses, their tack decorated with baronial crowns. Sitting on the coachman's box was a man dressed in parrot-coloured livery who sneered whenever he turned round and looked at his mistress. The baroness was a very strange-looking woman, common in the extreme yet decked out in all the finery of the last regency period.

Since no real negotiations could take place until they had seen the house, Törner and his wife accepted the invitation to accompany the baroness in her carriage out to the property, seven miles out of town on the high road between Landskrona and Hälsingborg.

As the party drove along the dirty highway Master Andreas Törner took the opportunity to study his future landlords more closely. The baroness had a sunburnt, round feline face with fish eyes and bad front teeth. She looked like a vegetable seller or a gardener's wife, without any hint of good breeding. The gardener or factor changed his expression every five minutes. His complexion was too pallid to be Scandinavian and his brown eyes, which had extremely dilated pupils, were fixed on the ground or to the side. His clothes were so ill-fitting that his tunic protruded above the collar of his cloak. Round his neck he wore a red velvet scarf with gold embroidery that looked as if it had been cut out of a chasuble or a cushion. His deerskin gloves were obviously too big and he pulled them off and on as if they embarrassed him; when he had finally taken them off and put them in his lap, Törner noticed a large diamond ring on his dirty, unwashed hand. The stone in the ring was far too big to be genuine even if the setting itself was real gold. His broad-brimmed hat was adorned with a completely inappropriate cock's feather and his wig looked as if it was woven from horsehair.

They drove in silence for a while until the baroness clearly felt duty-bound to be sociable, but the noise of the carriage made it impossible to hear what she was saying and Törner could do no more than stare at her ugly smile and black teeth, listen to a voice made hoarse by too many late nights, and sense her chilling glances fixed on him. He would have liked to look out of the window but it was too low and, since he was jammed into the seat right opposite this forty-year-old woman, he was forced to look her in the eye and show by the expression on his face that he was listening to her prattle. The landscape on both sides of the road was ravaged and desolate. They passed the ruins of castles and half-burnt windmills with their internal mechanisms exposed to the clear spring air. Since the most obvious topics of conversation were likely to endanger harmony, they fell back on renewed silence as the safest solution. After an hour's journey the coach approached a large beech-wood which extended across the low ridge between Landskrona and Hälsingborg and a quarter of an hour later they came to a halt at a tall iron gate hanging on stout stone pillars decorated with obelisks and balls.

The party climbed down and the baroness rang an old dinner

bell. The ringing was answered by dull barking that seemed to come from somewhere beneath them – repeated barks, strangely muffled as if from a hunt far away in the forest. The factor turned away with a troubled look but the coachman made no attempt to conceal his grin, as if he had done something bad. The baroness rang once more and at last a funny little fourteen-year-old boy of debauched appearance arrived. He looked like a blackamoor and was struggling to stop himself laughing.

Törner, hearing the mysterious howling again, took the liberty of asking whether they kept many dogs in the house and the baroness, true to the custom of the place, answered him with a question:

'Don't you like dogs?'

'I detest dogs,' he replied.

'That's good then, as we've only got one guard dog and it's always kept chained; and then there's a little one that lies on the bed all day,' the baroness answered, accommodating as ever. The coachman grinned with no attempt at restraint and the blackamoor boy looked as if he were grief-stricken.

Meanwhile the gate had opened and they were walking through an avenue of black spruce-trees towards the castle. It was a dark, rather unpretentious building with two wings and to judge from its appearance it might once have been the residence of the district governor. At the corners, however, four attic rooms had been built on in the form of towers, and over the dilapidated steps a porch had been added in an unrecognizable style. Everything was in disrepair. The gutters were leaking and the whitewash was peeling off the walls. Some of the bow-windows were painted green, others white, as if the paint had run out. At basement level they had, randomly as it were, knocked a window right through the middle of the frontage and a carpenter's bench and tools were visible inside. All along the avenue they had been wading through filth and it lay there in heaps in front of the door. The doorposts were filthy, the window panes were filthy, the lock on the door was filthy. Törner made a sign to his wife that they should turn back. But it was too late and, not wanting to insult their hosts, they stepped into a squalid hallway after wasting half an hour looking for the key. A stench of rotting meat or wet dogs met them as they entered. A narrow wooden staircase that had evidently not been scrubbed for years led up to the living quarters. The banister was hanging loose but was covered with red velvet held in place with brass tacks, though the velvet only reached halfway up the stairs. The last section of the banister was bare and dirty brown, daubed with home-made paint of some sort and showing the prints of dirty hands.

When the party reached the landing on the floor above they were forced to climb over paint pots, beer barrels, builders' trowels and scrap iron in order to proceed any further.

Master Törner was furious and wanted to leave but was immediately inundated with a catalogue of excuses about repairs and the like. Then, all at once, they found themselves in a large and splendid room filled with sunlight and Törner's mood brightened, especially when he saw a door leading out onto a balcony formed by the porch over the main door.

The room was panelled in oak to head height, the ceiling plastered with arabesques and decorated with paintings, and the polished prisms of an old chandelier split the rays of the sun into all the colours of the rainbow, which then shone on a massive stove-hood decorated with a broken coat of arms. The furnishings, mainly damaged musical instruments, did not match the decoration of the stately room. Scattered in various parts of the room were a crippled piano with very few remaining strings, a harp strung with hempen cords, a lute, a violin and a bassoon. Two half empty glasses had left rings on the shabby table and alongside them lay bread crusts and bacon rind – the remnants of a meal eaten off the corner of the dirty table.

The floor was streaked with clay and mud and marked with the imprints of clogs. But what made being in the room particularly unpleasant was the indescribably penetrating stench: it was the same combination of dishwater, dirty linen, old clothes, rotting meat and wet dogs that Törner had already noticed on the staircase. Choking on the foul air he opened the door to the balcony and let the spring wind flow in. The baroness, who had noticed the unfavourable impression the house was making, departed to fetch a glass of wine while the factor, now unconstrained by witnesses, gave free rein to his tongue.

The mansion had been built by the Danish king Kristian IV, the factor explained, and His Majesty had occupied this very room, which was why it was called the King's Room. The baroness's grandfather, one of King Kristian's courtiers, had received a grant of the mansion along with its tenant farms. After the Swedish conquest of the province he had, of course, been forced to give up the tenant farms. Nowadays the baroness owned only this estate but she also received large sums of money from interest on her capital. She lived a retired life and never socialized with her neighbours: she could not tolerate Danes because her mother was Russian. There were other reasons too, apparently, but the factor seemed unable to explain them. His point, however, was that there was no animosity towards Swedes in this house – quite the reverse. The factor himself had never prospered as much as he did under Swedish rule whereas the Danes in the district hated and detested him, the reasons for which he did not want to go into.

After viewing the other rooms in the apartment they returned to the King's Room where the baroness had already settled down with a jug of wine and glasses. While the wine was being poured the factor went unnoticed over to a large clock standing by the wall and pulled a string that made it play an Italian minuet. Then they drank the wine. Master Törner turned away and spat it out on the balcony while the factor lauded the wine as genuine and claimed to have ordered it direct from France – a statement that was impossible to contest though Törner thought it tasted of rotten apples.

After some brief negotiations about the price of the apartment, which was so low there was little room for disagreement, they went to the floor above to view the room that would be Törner's study. To their great surprise they had to pick their way through an attic filled with all kinds of household junk – chests, furniture, ironware, wooden objects, pottery, clothes, rags, broken glassware, door and window frames, slates, tools – all kinds of things, and all of them damaged in some way.

They were no less surprised on entering the tower rooms. There were wardrobes with costumes from the time of Gustav I onwards – hats, wigs, sunshades, chests, reliquaries, books and papers. After viewing three rooms Master Törner wanted to move on to the fourth but was informed that the factor occupied that one and no-one knew where the key was. Having settled on one of the available rooms – always assuming they decided to rent the place at all – they went down to the garden. It covered a large area, with numerous fruit trees and berry bushes. The beds were edged with low boxwood hedges and there were pergolas, summerhouses and lawns. In the middle of the park there was a carp lake in which there were said to be all kinds of fish, even pike, though that seemed unlikely to Törner if there were supposed to be carp and crayfish there too. A bridge led out to a temple on the lake. The remains of a marble fountain stood beside it, along with the pediment of a statue, a broken Delft urn and a piece of a sundial. Everything was in a state of decay. The trees had grown together and were already overshadowing everything even though the leaves had not yet come out. The paths were overgrown, the trellises rotten and everywhere was a wilderness of weeds. But the factor had answers ready for all their adverse comments. He pointed out rightly enough that no garden looked at its best until it had been tidied and dug over. The winter snows had put paid to most of it but now that spring was on its way three gardeners were due to arrive and things would soon be different. Törner was a reasonable man and, when he saw a hothouse in which melons were already beginning to trail among all kinds of flowering plants and where the chervil was an inch high, he fell in love with the place.

After viewing the garden they returned to the King's Room where the women had been conversing about domestic matters. The factor filled the wine-glasses and the baroness brought out a small chest from which she took a hurdy-gurdy and, kneeling in front of it, began to play a well-known gavotte from Queen

Kristina's ballet. Meanwhile, the factor vanished.

Master Andreas Törner and his wife sat there exchanging glances filled with amazement at these strange people. In whispered undertones they commented on all the mysterious things they had seen and heard. A baroness on her knees in the dirt playing a hurdy-gurdy, dressed like a gipsy, unwashed, uncombed, oblivious to the errand that had brought her guests to the place, draining glass after glass like a drunkard – it was, to say the least, an unusual sight.

While they are sitting there thinking about all this the little blackamoor enters carrying a table covered with a dirty cloth. He puts it down in the middle of the room and fills it with a variety of strange-looking objects. The factor appears dressed in a conjurer's outfit and holding a magic wand.

Törner is now convinced he has come to a madhouse but his suspicions are interrupted by the factor who explains in boastful tones that, in addition to his duties on the estate, he is a conjurer and has performed as such in the great cities of Europe, where he enjoyed huge success.

The baroness continues playing the hurdy-gurdy and accompanies the factor in a a song about a certain Count of Luxembourg, believed to be in league with the devil as well as with poisoners. The factor's appearance has changed completely from that of the humble gardener and he is now singing, rushing round and gesticulating like a savage with rolling eyes and huge white flashing teeth.

'He looks like an incarnation of the devil himself,' Mistress Törner whispered to her husband and wanted to leave but Master Törner, not in normal circumstances a nervous man, advised against any breach with their hosts since it was impossible to know whether they were among madmen or bandits.

Then the factor changes his mask and, with exaggerated gestures, begins behaving like a lovable conjurer. He is prepared to wager anything they care to name that he can conjure a mug of mulled wine out of his hat. Törner knows that trick (and a good many more difficult ones too) but he puts a brave face on it, accepts the wager and plays the part of the baffled onlooker. The mulled wine duly makes its appearance and the factor boasts about his skill while the baroness claps her hands in wonder.

By now the sun has gone down and evening is wearing on. Master Törner begs leave to depart in order to get home before night and the factor orders the horses to be harnessed. But while they are waiting for the carriage to drive up, the conjurer spins out one trick after another, all of them of the tawdriest kind – the sort performed by market entertainers. An hour passes and the carriage has still not appeared. Then Törner gets angry and says he wants to leave even if it means renting a carriage from the nearest inn. His wife has been sitting there shivering with cold and, being of a sickly disposition, she has begun to suspect they have been lured into a trap. The factor becomes chivalrous, helps the lady on with her cloak, fills the glasses yet again and while doing so carelessly puts his arm round the baroness's waist. She seems to be drunk. Twilight has fallen and they part without having come to any firm decision about the accommodation though Törner has promised to give them his answer within a week.

When they are on the stairs they hear again the subterranean barking of dogs and when Törner stops and listens he is startled by a scream from the yard – the scream of a terrified child or a dying fox or a woman in childbirth.

'What was that?' he asked, turning to the factor.

'What?' the factor asked, sticking firmly to the habit of the house and not answering.

'Didn't you hear a scream?'

'No.'

Master Törner took a firm grip of his hawthorn stick and stared at the man to see whether he was lying. And then he went down the steps. The carriage had been driven up and the coachman with the permanent leer stood alongside and had great difficulty in not bursting into laughter as he pretended to dry off the horses with the arm of his smock. Törner now noticed that the horses were nothing but skin and bone. Their hide – originally white – was almost yellow and covered with big black, brown and reddish-yellow patches, and they were festooned with lumps of dirt.

Accompanied by a flood of assurances from the factor that this was the best, the cheapest, the quietest place they would find, Törner and his wife drove off, firmly resolved never to set foot in the house again.

*

The following morning Master Andreas Törner went to see the stallholder who had told him about the accommodation at Bögely to try to get some reliable information about the place. The stallholder smiled and admitted that the people there were a bit strange and eccentric but added that nothing bad had ever been heard about them. The man was of gipsy origin, had come to the baroness as coachman, then risen to factor before finally becoming her lover. Her father had also been an eccentric who went round dressed in clogs and rags and her mother had suffered periods of mental confusion. It had, moreover, been an unhappy marriage and the baroness's parents had consequently put a clause in their will that stipulated she should never marry. Should she do so, she would lose her inheritance.

This information was all Törner needed and he put the whole business out of his mind as being of no further interest.

But the image of the dark house returned to him with all the power of things mysterious and unusual so that, when spring arrived in earnest in the first days of May and his efforts to find suitable accommodation had still not met with success, he made a sudden decision to rent Bögely, attracted mainly perhaps by his memories of the extensive old garden in which he expected to find rare plants of interest both to his field of research and as *materia medica*.

So, when the storks arrived and the nightingales began to sing, Master Törner gathered his family and possessions, moved out of town and settled into the strange house.

Everything there was in the same state as before and a week was spent scrubbing, sweeping and tidying. Everything was dilapidated. There were no window catches and some panes had been replaced with sheets of tin. Doors hung on one hinge and all the locks were broken so they had to sleep with the doors unlocked. But since Törner now knew that the people of the house were decent people in good circumstances he did not harbour any suspicions and, after having vainly repeated his request for a locksmith to be sent for, he simply accepted the carelessness.

On his walks in the garden during these beautiful spring days, however, he made one discovery after another that reinforced his conviction that he was not only dealing with a half-mad individual but also with a liar. He noticed how day by day the number of dogs increased so that after eight days there were eight large or small dogs roaming around, lying on the steps and barking at the sun, the wind, the crows or anything else that came in sight. And all of them looked starved, like badly stuffed exhibits in the Zoological Museum. It was evident that the people of the house had lied shamelessly and Törner would have been furious had Jensen not seemed so deferential and made every effort to be kind and helpful in other respects.

The stables were separated from the house by a yard. It was a showpiece of disorder. The animals were all mixed together as in Noah's Ark: two heifers as thin as long-tailed monkeys, a cow without an udder, three decrepit nags, hens, ducks, turkeys. On the roof of the privy that bordered one side of the yard they had built a rabbit pen, with bars to protect them from the dogs.

Although both Jensen and the baroness were constantly insisting on their boundless love for animals, the beasts were hardly given anything to eat. The horses chewed chaff with no oats, the cow licked moss or the mould on the walls or pulled down straw from the rotten thatch of the roof, and the poultry fought over dung. There was no bedding in the stables and the animals slept on their own excrement. In the midst of all this misery, however, two peacocks paraded around and showed off their finery to the envious turkeys, which were quick to attack them.

Master Törner continued his exploration and arrived at the cellar window at the front of the house where he had noticed the carpenter's bench. Looking down through the window he was met by the happy leering face of the coachman and, in the half-darkness behind it, another face with a red beard.

'What on earth! Have you got a carpenter's workshop here?' Master Törner asked, surprised to see the coachman standing there in full livery with a plane in his hand.

'What haven't we got!' Madsen answered with a crafty look. 'But no-one's meant to know about it, though.'

'Who takes care of the land and the animals?'

'Ivan, I suppose.'

'Who's Ivan?'

'The factor's brother, or so they say.'

'The small chap?'

'Yes.'

'So the factor isn't a farmer then?' Törner asked again, more and more confused by this household full of surprises.

'The factor is supposed to be a chairmaker,' Madsen answered, at which a roar of laughter came from the cellar.

Not wishing to become the confidant or accomplice of underlings, Törner cut short his questioning and went out into the garden. It was now well into the month of May but the earth had not yet been touched by a spade. The weeds had grown tall and the coltsfoot had finished flowering and gone to seed. When he reached the hothouse he saw that the melons were dried up and weeds a foot high hid the flowering plants. Törner was shocked that a couple of months' work should be allowed to go to waste in this way and he opened the door and went in to save what could be saved. Only when he went down into it did he discover that it wasn't a brick hothouse at all but a wooden shed built over a mound of earth and covered with straw and soil. The wind and rain had free entry. There was a heating system and a stove but they were laughable, and the glass had been removed from the frames so the seedbeds lay there uncovered, untended and unsown.

Törner began to pull up the weeds but before he had pulled up more than a handful he felt something cold and unpleasant touch his neck. He turned round quickly, stepping aside at the same time, and caught sight of a large black grass-snake hanging from the roof and flicking its outstretched tongue. He raised his spade to kill the creature but at that moment he heard an anxious voice imploring him from over by the door.

'No, don't! For pity's sake don't kill my snake!' It was the factor.

'Why not?' Törner asked in amazement.

'Because grass-snakes are sacred creatures and they bring good luck.'

'There's no such thing as sacred creatures these days,' Törner answered, being a secret disciple of the philosophy of Descartes. 'And if it's supposed to bring good luck, there's certainly no sign of it in here. Why didn't you water the melons?'

The factor thought for a moment before answering:

'Well, they're actually a variety that doesn't need water.'

'What variety is that?'

'Haarlem melons,' answered the factor, quick to come up with a response.

Törner, forced to admit his own ignorance, said nothing.

It was not until they came out of the hothouse that he noticed the factor had shaved off his beard, revealing full lips around which there was a network of playful lines. He was wearing a yellow velvet jacket, blue scarf, red stockings and a blond wig, as well as a peculiar cap with a peacock feather of the sort normally only worn by horse-traders. He was almost unrecognizable.

Master Törner walked through the garden with him pointing to the devastation all round and asking whether he intended to dig the ground over soon.

Of course, he was! It was going to look fantastic once he'd got hold of the right master gardener from Rosenborg in Copenhagen, though he wasn't available just yet.

They crossed two long beds in which some tall green stalks were sticking up among the burdock and willowherb. They caught

Törner's attention.

'Good Lord! Are you letting asparagus shoot up without covering it?' he exclaimed. 'Can't you be bothered to do anything?'

The factor drummed his chin with his fingers, pushed out his top lip in an attempt to look knowledgeable and answered:

'Well, we aren't going to harvest it this year. It's better if you leave it alone for one summer.'

'I've heard that it goes woody if it's not tended and cut,' Törner objected.

'Mm, maybe that's what happens farther north,' the factor said, never short of an answer. 'But things might well be different in the loose soil down here.'

And so they walked on. When they had finished with the garden and reached the fields, there was a new surprise awaiting the astonished academic. A smooth field of beautiful soil stretched as far as the eye could see but four-fifths of it lay fallow and covered in weeds. Some of the rest was under grass, one section showed some mixed crops and Ivan was busy harrowing the last piece.

Trying to avoid a critical tone, Master Törner risked another question.

'Have you sown anything yet?'

'No,' the factor answered quickly, as was his habit, but with neither the intention nor the ability to come up with fresh excuses. 'No, we always do the sowing late so the seed won't lie there and rot.'

'That's very strange,' Törner replied. 'Is it some new method?'

'Yes, absolutely new.'

They walked on out through the fields and stopped at the green fodder. It was a mixture of rye and wheat, thistles and chicory, turnips and peas – even leeks. Törner laughed to himself but avoided tackling the subject head on.

'Where did you learn your agriculture?' he asked, simply to ask something.

An uncomfortable silence followed.

'I learnt it on Count Bille-Brahe's estate on Fyn.'

'And you work the farm without hired help?'

'I work it myself, along with Ivan. He's a real worker, small as he is.'

'Who's Ivan?' Törner asked to see how far the factor would go in his foolish effrontery.

'He's a poor crofter's son from near Landskrona and I've given him a leg up,' the gipsy answered.

The harrow drove past at that moment, bouncing across the unploughed soil with Ivan lying on top with the reins round his neck singing at the top of his voice.

Master Törner had seen enough, but he was still unable to work out what kind of people he was dealing with. Were they madmen, bandits, or both?

*

Meanwhile the baroness did not appear for several weeks. She was said to be unwell, which did not prevent the sounds of music and singing coming from her room half the night. And Törner noticed that they never heard the factor going up to his attic room. On one occasion, when trying to get to the bottom of the whole business, he asked Ivan where the factor lived and he pointed to a first-floor window – precisely the apartment occupied by the baroness. There was an entrance to it from the hallway that led to Törner's own apartments. The door to her rooms, however, was always closed and when Törner or one of his family knocked to ask for anyone the door was opened just a crack – and even then only after hammering on it for a long time. The message would be taken through the crack to the accompaniment of the wild clamour of a pack of dogs. Anyone who managed to peep in could see nothing because it was pitch black in there and, in any case, they were driven back by the unbearable smell.

One day when the Törners were sitting in their drawing room they heard a cock crowing behind the closed door of the baroness's apartment. Their maid claimed she had even heard kids bleating and turtledoves cooing in there but, having once decided to come to Bögely and the contract being binding until the first day of October, they made it a rule to keep their noses out of other people's business and to avoid stirring up ill-feeling and suspicion by enquiring too closely.

Despite this resolution, however, Master Törner struggled to overcome his curiosity. Educated as a researcher he was in the habit of never giving up until he got to the bottom of things, and anything and everything that seemed inexplicable at first sight only served to fan the flames of his desire for an explanation. This mysterious house and its peculiar inhabitants had that effect on him. A baroness with a fortune who nevertheless liked living in filth and discomfort; an animal lover who starved her animals. And a gipsy who was a chairmaker, odd-job man, conjurer, gardener and farmer but who could not even put a latch on a window, could not do tricks properly and did not know when to sow rye; who lied every time he opened his mouth; who went round in fancy dress and changed his appearance twice a day. There was plenty of digging to be done here and plenty to be explained. Since Törner had a view of the yard, garden and fields from his window in the tower and since his window was immediately above that of the baroness, his opportunities for observation and listening were good. And since part of his task was to acquaint himself with the opinions of the populace, he had no difficulty in calming any twinges of conscience about snooping into their secrets – particularly as he had no intention of using what he discovered for anything but his own amusement.

*

One morning in June, with the clock coming up to eleven and the sun high, Master Törner was lying in his tower window smoking his pipe. It had been a stormy night down in the baroness's room as the factor had been singing, playing and drinking well into the small hours. Then things had gone quiet – in the apartment downstairs, that is, but not out in the back yard. The horses in the stable were stamping and biting their cribs with hunger, the cow

37

was bellowing, the goats bleating, the cocks crowing, the turkeys gobbling, the peacocks screeching as if possessed. And all this had been going on since daybreak six hours earlier.

A window opened at last and the factor's black chicken-thief's wig sticks out and a moment later his yellow jerkin is visible down in the yard. First of all he opens a little hatch for the hens, which emerge at a frantic speed, so eager to get out into the sunlight that they jam in the hatch two by two, after which they storm the dung-hill. Then the ducks waddle up, wash their necks in some brown liquid that has collected in the wheel tracks and then lay siege to the dung-hill, whence they drive the hens by pecking their backsides. For a short time the peacocks are merely arrogant spectators of the ducks' mopping-up operation. Then they too storm the dung-hill, flip the ducks' beaks with their long tail feathers and nip them in the neck with their predatory beaks.

Once they have taken possession of the top of the hill, they raise their flags, strut round and round in triumph, clap their chocolate-brown under-wings and trumpet a challenge to the turkeys. The turkeys are quick to take them up on it and the two cocks bend their necks back, pump red blood into their wattles, spread their wings like shields and run up onto the soft rampart. But they have trouble turning and so make a flanking attack using their wings and spurs. And the peacocks, when they cannot hold their ground, rise in a little hopping flight – but do not surrender the dung-hill.

The factor, having let the horses out, takes a whip and brings the turkeys under control with a couple of quick lashes at their wattles.

The horses walk round nosing for wisps of straw but fail to find any. The cow comes out and immediately lies down. The goats gnaw at the privy door, which is made of strips of beech nailed together with the bark still on. The whole yard is a confused jumble of animals.

The factor takes a scythe from the ground and goes out into the fields and Törner can see him swiping at the half-grown rye until he has mown a little heap which he loads onto a cart. Ivan, who has now arrived, helps him cart it back to the yard. What a commotion that causes! The horses bite and kick, the cow gets up, and the goats stand on their hind-legs to tear down whatever they can reach.

Meanwhile the factor goes up on the roof of the privy with an armful of greenery for the rabbits, after which he lies out flat in the sunshine whip in hand, cracking it lightly over the heads of the animals whenever their fighting becomes too ill-tempered.

Now the baroness emerges in a sky-blue dress, an amber necklace around her bare neck and clogs on her feet. She is carrying a washing-up bowl into which she is going to milk the cow. She has neither combed her hair nor washed and she scratches her head now and then as if trying to untangle her thoughts. The cow kicks and refuses to release any milk but the milking has to be done anyway, and when the baroness expresses surprise at her lack of success the factor answers crossly – but without moving from where he is lying – that the cow is probably in calf and thus incapable of giving milk. The baroness carries out a superficial check but fails to reach any conclusion. Then the yard goes quiet again and the factor falls asleep up on the privy roof, whip still in hand.

Törner, who was directly above the sleeping man, was now able to study his face while it was not under the watchful control of his waking will. It was marked by a deathly pallor, wild lines that seemed at war with one another, deep furrows as if hollowed out by sins and passions. His eyeballs were large and their shape could be discerned under his eyelids which, when closed, concealed the anxiety that lurked behind them. The rabbits crept round the sleeping man, nosed at him and then scuttled back under their planks. They re-emerged, sniffed at his clothes and wrinkled their noses, flipped their ears and put them together when they heard the drunken moaning of the sleeping factor.

Törner had studied the man quite long enough to think he had good reason to believe the factor to be an out-and-out thief and liar. He had followed all of Törner's advice about gardening and agriculture without ever admitting where it had come from and without a word of thanks. He had both watered and cut the melons as Törner had suggested and then boasted of his own wisdom. He had pruned the asparagus and, with a look of triumph, shown Törner that he knew how to grow asparagus. Törner had put a good face on it as usual but wondered how a gipsy who thought himself to be so cunning could be stupid enough to believe that Törner neither remembered nor understood anything. On the other hand, the factor behaved towards Törner with the sort of dog-like devotion that is shown to a generous benefactor. Or to someone to whom one ascribes a high degree of altruism and honour – and thus feels at liberty to cheat. The gipsy loved him, or claimed to do so, and respected him as a man who unselfishly shared his superior knowledge – knowledge that could be turned to economic advantage. Having grown up among thieves and rogues he bowed before a man he believed incapable of lying, but his admiration also contained an element of sympathy for someone who did not have the sense to see through the deceitfulness of others. And true to his thieving nature he could not desist from deceiving his altruistic benefactor and friend. Thus Master Törner had discovered that the wine the factor boasted of importing from France was actually apple-wine he had pressed himself from rotten fruit and the juice that ran out was thick and brown like Spanish Alicante – which the factor confused with a French wine. If Törner asked the factor to buy groceries for him he always brought home spoilt items at the highest prices. Permission to pick a few sprigs of the parsley that was growing half wild among the weeds in the garden cost Törner three times as much as in the market in Lund. And then there was the host of trivial things the factor had contracted to do but failed to carry out. All in all, Törner thought he had quite enough evidence to condemn the man. But he still did not get angry with the wretch. Since he was well aware that the ruling environment, together with upbringing, racial predetermination and national character all exert an influence on human nature, he was glad to have the chance to study the role-play of this pariah who had dragged himself out of poverty and achieved a certain social status by forming a relationship with a branch of a family that claimed both antiquity and nobility.

At noon, after Törner had eaten and gone up to his room in the tower, the factor was still lying peacefully asleep among the rabbits. He was wakened by the noise of Törner's window, rubbed his eyes, shouted for Ivan and ordered all the horses to be hitched to the roller. Then he jumped down from the roof, took a sack of seed and went out to the field.

For some time Törner watched the ridiculous sight of the gipsy in his yellow jacket sowing the unploughed field that Ivan had harrowed, leaving the thistles lying there with their roots in the air. He walked with a solemn gait, making sweeping conjurer's gestures with his hands as he broadcast seed, his lips moving as if he was reciting something. After walking up and down for half an hour he stopped, apparently tired, whistled to Ivan who drove up with the roller pulled by three horses, swung himself up into the seat, took the reins and cracked the whip. The scene beggared belief: the gipsy on the roller in his Brabant hat with its peacock feather; the skeletal horses in gleaming harness with the shining coat of arms and plumes – there being only one set of harness for all purposes; and the team of three horses dragging the roller at a gallop like a gun carriage on its way into action. The work was finished in a quarter of an hour.

It was just before midsummer and here was the gipsy sowing an unploughed field with two bushels of oats.

After these exertions he went down to the summerhouse on the lake and called for a mug of beer. He sat there with it watching the carp for three hours. Then he ordered up a horse and rode off at a trot down to the coast.

When the evening sun was close to setting and Törner had eaten his supper he usually went down to the garden alone since his wife was a chronic invalid and the children went to bed early. He found it distressing to walk round the dirty overgrown garden and the only clean and dry place to retire to was the summerhouse on the lake. He had spent a month trying to catch the pike he had been told about until one day Ivan let it slip that there never had been any pike there, nor crayfish. This made little impression on

Törner since he knew what to expect from the factor by now.

Sitting there listening to the song of the nightingale in the currant bushes and feeling ill at ease with the unbearable filth and desolation all round him, he heard a noisy song approaching through the darkness of the avenue of maple trees and the factor's yellow jerkin showed up in the red light of the declining sun.

'I am the Count of Luxembourg, tralala, lalala!' he sang at the top of his voice and greeted Törner with all the elegance of a courtier, though grotesquely exaggerated. His face was very pale, as if he had been involved in a serious brawl. His eyes rolled and flashed and his lips were a blue-black colour. Ivan was walking behind him dressed as a page and wearing a sword at his side. He was carrying a tray with a wine jug and some greenish-yellow glasses.

Master Törner looked anxiously at the awful wine and the dirty glasses but neither wished nor dared to refuse the invitation.

The factor seemed excited and rather drunk. His speech at first was loud and arrogant.

'Ah, Master Törner, you're having a tedious time of it but soon the master gardener from Kristiansborg will be here and then things will be different. He's the finest gardener in the whole of Scandinavia and I'll pay him a hundred daler a month over and above his board,' the factor boasted.

'Tell me something,' Andreas Törner interrupted. 'Isn't there anyone at all in the whole district whose company is worth keeping?'

'Not a soul,' the gipsy assured him. 'Rabble, the lot of them! Rabid Swede-haters! No, believe me Master Törner, you shouldn't throw your lot in with them. I am your friend because in a way I'm Swedish too. My paternal grandmother was Swedish and my grandfather French – and the French are superior to all other nations. Deep down I feel I'm a born Frenchman but with Swedish blood in my veins. And I hate the Danes, I hate them!' he screamed and rose to his feet with bloodshot eyes. 'And they hate me in return. I promise you that,' he hissed with conviction.

Ivan, who had returned with a silver serving-jug, put it down on the table and sat down. When the factor noticed this he raised his hand and gave the boy such a clout that he flew up from the bench.

'Stand there, you dog!' he roared when Ivan seemed about to leave. 'Stand there and hold the jug!'

Törner decided to let the gipsy ramble on and reveal his secrets yet again. But in order to lull any suspicions he put on an expression of approval and sympathy, uttered some meaningless words of encouragement and played the part of the attentive listener – the grateful pupil who listens reverently to the incomparable wisdom of the man of experience.

'*Maxima desetur pueris reverentia*, or, to translate, children owe their elders the greatest respect,' he quoted in support of the gipsy's shameful treatment of his brother.

The gipsy walked into the trap and, after emptying another glass, opened his heart.

'I am of humble origins, as you know, Master Törner. But I have talent, and people can't stand that. I was a journeyman shoemaker in Copenhagen and when I was only seventeen I was the most skilful of the lot. But I couldn't get into a guild because I was too young. And when I set up shop anyway, the police and the alderman came to close me down. I went berserk and hurled the lot of them out, using one to hit the other until the guard arrived and threw me in the lock-up. Then they thought they'd got me but I was smarter than them and went to the royal council, indeed, to the king himself, and both the policeman and the alderman were forced to stand there with long faces while I got off. The police have hated me ever since but can't do anything about it. No-one can touch a hair of my head, and if anyone dares try he's as good as dead. I admit I've been to gaol but I've never been found guilty of anything. Never. And you, being a gentleman, will take my word for it, won't you? Because I love you as a brother, as a friend! I love you because you're the first person to treat me as a human being. You don't know how malicious the neighbours have been from the moment I moved into this district! Nothing but trouble and provocation. At one moment they're tearing down my fences and letting their animals in, at the next they're like thieving ravens. They put rocks out in the road so my horses get hurt. And I've never done them anything but good! I don't know how many thousand I've lent them interest free, and I never get a penny back. The baroness, who has a heart of pure gold (this he shouted so it could be heard up at the house), has fed and clothed the local paupers year in and year out and they're still not ashamed to rob her. She's an angel, a pure and just woman without a stain on her character, but they slander her grossly. Oh, so grossly! It's just envy, you see, envy because she won't mix with them, just shuts herself away with the animals she loves more than anything else. Animals, Master Törner, they're so much better than people, so much better! They are grateful, they know how to value a good deed. Unlike people! Oh, how worthless mankind is!'

All this talking and ranting had made him foam at the mouth and Törner, who already knew how to interpret his lies, felt he had a considerably clearer picture of the man than before.

At a sign from the gipsy Ivan fetched the hurdy-gurdy and placed it on the stone bench. The factor, in a much brighter frame of mind now he believed he had dispelled all Törner's suspicions, felt the need to give free rein to his happiness by demonstrating his superiority in the musical sphere while also taking the opportunity to add a touch of mystery to his person. Something which, in fact, was notably lacking or, if it did exist, only did so in a very crude form.

In a coarse, piercing singing voice (which resembled the yells of a market-trader more than anything else) and wearing an expression intended to hint at something mysterious, he began to perform his favourite song while Ivan wound the handle of the hurdy-gurdy.

> Oh, I am the Count of Luxembourg,
> Tralalala lalala.
> By day and night with dog and horn
> I make my way through forest deep

And sing my song up on the hill.
Whoever hears my horn falls still
For I've made a pact with the Devil!

There followed numerous stanzas concerning this once notorious Marshal and Count of Luxembourg and his mysterious life among bandits and poisoners, as well as his miraculous rescue from the clutches of the police and the witchcraft commissioners.

Intoxicated by wine and song the gipsy began to grow sentimental and, in a fit of magnanimity, offered his glass to Ivan who emptied it with bared head and bent knee as befits a page. He did this with some grace despite his pitiably starved appearance and Törner felt it proper to reward him with an encouraging nod. At which the gipsy could no longer control his joy and pride and, forgetting his earlier lies, he blurted out a revelation.

'He's my brother, you know, Master Törner. I'm bringing him up strictly and he's going to be a great man, perhaps an Admiral of the Realm even, if we're spared.'

Törner at once began to discourse enthusiastically on the rapid development of naval power in Scandinavia and the brilliant career prospects currently available in that noble profession. He offered sound advice on how a young man should behave, which paths he should follow and what knowledge he must acquire, in order to advance as a naval officer.

Meanwhile night had fallen but the bright summer sky still gave enough light for Törner to see the baroness come creeping along the avenue of maple trees. The factor had already caught sight of her and, hat in hand, went to meet her on the bridge, bade her welcome and asked whether she would take a glass of wine in the company of Master Törner. The baroness thanked him, sat down and drank from the same glass as the factor as is the custom among the peasantry. She already seemed tipsy. The gipsy had no idea how to deport himself: he wanted to show himself in an honourable light by being as respectful as possible to his mistress and, at the same time, wanted to demonstrate how close his relationship with the noble lady was. Which could only be revealed by committing indiscretions that risked being discourteous. So at one moment he was handing her a glass with bent knee and bared head and the next he was putting his arm around her waist in an intimate manner. And sometimes he addressed her respectfully as 'Your Grace', sometimes casually as 'you' – an alternation that made him sound quite ridiculous.

After the baroness had spent some time boasting of her noble ancestors who had served Kristian IV – clearly the only king she and the factor had heard of – she asked the gipsy, whom she called Jensen, to sing about the Count of Luxembourg.

The Count of Luxembourg seemed to haunt the pair of them to a degree that made Törner concerned for their sanity. When the gipsy sang the song yet again, all the while casting glances of secret understanding in the direction of the baroness, she laughed uproariously as if he had come up with something clever and, when the song was finished, she asked Törner whether he liked it. The latter replied that Jensen was worthy of a place in the royal choir, where he would undoubtedly become a great and eminent singer. At which the gipsy, beside himself with joy, sang a song about Eulenspiegel and, when he had finished that, recited – without waiting to be asked – the whole of the tale of Fortunatus and his magic hat. Törner found the whole performance unbearable and asked himself how he could sit there listening calmly to such a conceited but untalented street-performer. Finally he rose and said goodnight, at which the party broke up and they all walked back together through the garden. The serpentine gait of the factor and the baroness revealed that they had indulged to excess and, there being numerous items to carry, Törner offered his assistance and took the wine flagon and the jug. When they entered the vestibule the baroness, throwing caution to the winds, opened her kitchen door and politely invited Törner to step in.

'It looks rather untidy in here,' she said by way of excuse, 'but you are a kind man and you must see my little animals.'

The sight that was then revealed to the unsuspecting visitor surpassed anything he could have imagined in his wildest dreams.

It was a real witch's kitchen. The walls, floor and ceiling shone black with soot. A long row of glass bottles and alchemist's retorts stood on top of the stove among pans and leftover food. Piles of turnips, cabbages and onions lay on the floor and a side of mutton was hanging on one wall, high enough to be out of reach of the dogs. The dogs ran round the arrivals, wagging their tails and sniffing at the stranger's stockings. A young man was lying under a sheet on a folding bench with only the back of his shaggy head visible. When the gipsy lit a tallow candle a cock flew up onto the headboard and began to crow.

'This is my favourite old pet,' said the baroness, stroking a multi-coloured creature in her lap. 'Have you ever seen a twenty-year-old, blind cockerel before?'

The ill-natured bird hacked at the finger Törner stretched out to tickle its neck.

Then another door was opened and they entered a smaller room. The first thing visible was an enormous bed with a canopy and curtains. Two yellow Great Danes were standing on the bed copulating and the other inhabitants were simply ignoring them. The only window in the room was occupied by cages full of siskin and turtledoves. A stuffed stork with outstretched wings hung from the ceiling, in its beak a dried viper. Two large thin dogs lay on the floor in a corner alongside a coop full of chickens, a cat with six kittens was sleeping in a basket, and the baroness produced a family of ducklings from a chest of drawers.

There was a foul stink of animals and the floor was filthy with excrement.

The baroness, who was showing off her beloved creatures, now went to open the door to a third room and, though the gipsy made any number of unambiguous gestures to stop her, she let Törner in. He found himself in a large room, so packed with furniture and objects of all kinds that there was hardly a clear space. It was difficult to place a foot on the floor without trampling on something as there were heaps of clothes and ribbons, books, engravings and maps. Goblets, vases and cooking pots stood in the windows. Cupboards, chairs and desks crowded the walls and were piled on top of each other so that the room looked more like a secondhand shop than a living room.

At the end of the tour Törner was invited to take a seat in the bedroom and drink a glass of wine of an even finer vintage and, since the night was already wasted and dawn was approaching, he thought it would be entertaining to watch these people divulge more of their secrets.

The gipsy filled the glasses and started boasting again, talking of his possessions, his estate and his animals. After continuing in this vein for a while, the demon of arrogance took hold of him and he wanted to sing, at which Törner, by now weary of playing the fool to such a tinker, tuned a lute that was lying there untouched and passed it to the gipsy, who pushed it away with an expression of displeasure and the humiliating admission that he could not play it. Törner then offered him the fiddle and the harp with the same result.

'Surely the baroness plays?' he asked, turning to her.

No, she did not.

To get his own back the factor asked scornfully whether Törner himself would like to play and the latter responded by playing a gavotte.

The factor listened respectfully enough but looked dejected and unpleasantly surprised, as if Törner had made a fool of him.

Then Törner sang, accompanying himself on the harp and then playing dances on the violin. Finally he told a story.

The baroness was ecstatic but the gipsy sat there like a wet and beaten dog. He waited, ready to seize any opportunity to take up the challenge with a song.

During a pause he leapt to his feet, cleared his throat and exclaimed:

'Now I'd like the chance to do a turn!'

'Just behave yourself and keep quiet about your Count of Luxembourg, Jensen!' the baroness interrupted.

The gipsy, bristling with envy and rage, sat down to wait for a chance to avenge himself.

'Oh yes, so Master Törner is a real magician, is he?' he exclaimed. 'But I bet he can't pull chickens out of a hat!'

'Can't I? Look, my dear Jensen, I know all your tricks and several more besides!' Törner answered jovially.

'Oh, this we must see, this we must see!' the baroness shouted and clapped her hands.

Törner let her plead for a while, after which he took a pen and a small bottle from his pocket and asked for a piece of writing paper. The liquid in the bottle was colourless and when he wrote it left no trace of writing on the paper. Then he sealed the letter with resin. Once he had done that he invited the gipsy to open the letter and read it.

The gipsy (who actually could read) went ashen-faced when he saw the word that emerged very clearly in blue ink. While the baroness tried in vain to work out its meaning, the gipsy and Törner exchanged a look that did not augur well.

'But what on earth does it say?' asked the baroness, becoming more and more curious.

'It's just a Latin word – Romani – which means Romans,' Master Törner replied, eyeing the gipsy to make it clear to him that he also knew that Romani was the gipsies' name for themselves.

The gipsy fought a mental struggle as to whether to concede or to resist this demolition of his superiority in the eyes of the baroness. But a fierce hunger to gain access to Törner's knowledge led him to concede.

'It must cost a great deal of money to get ink like that,' he said in a voice both sullen and subservient.

'No, it doesn't cost anything at all,' Törner answered. 'Go down to the garden yourself, pick some marigolds and press out the juice.'

'Marigolds?' the gipsy repeated. 'But what spell do you have to recite?'

'Spell? Oh, I see. Do you seriously think I'd have any truck with spells and incantations? I'll tell you something, Jensen, if I'd really wanted to pretend to possess occult knowledge I wouldn't have shown you the bottle and I'd have had a piece of paper written on in advance. And when I showed you the white paper

I'd have simply lied to you that there was nothing written on it – and then I'd have recited some nonsense like *pax + max + nis + skaris*. But I showed you the marigold juice instead, and I'll tell you quite openly that one property of marigold juice is that it goes blue on contact with the heat of the seal. Why it goes blue is beyond me, I just know that it does!'

The gipsy could not understand why anyone would reveal such valuable tricks: they could, after all, be used for secret documents. But what really tormented his soul was that he had come off worse in a contest in which he had been allowed to delude himself that he was the stronger. Suddenly he leapt to his feet, took a dirty pack of cards from his pocket and shrieked:

'Pay attention now, Master Törner. I'm going to tell your fortune.'

'You can't,' Törner answered in a polite but superior tone.

'I can't?' hissed the gipsy, who fancied himself to be a master of the art.

'No, you can't – absolutely can't!' Törner assured him. 'And the reason you can't do it is because you don't know me, don't know my parents, my wife, my children, nor my ancestors – and part of my destiny depends on all of these. You can't because you have no idea of what I know or am capable of. You can't because you have no understanding of what's going on out in the world these days, and you don't know the forces that govern a man's fate. But I can tell your fortune without any cards and without any mumbo-jumbo. Do you believe me?'

The gipsy had sunk down on a chair and his body writhed like a snake under the heel of a boot.

'Hm! So? You can tell my fortune?' he flared up again.

'Yes, because I know you,' Törner answered in a quiet but definite voice.

'You? You – you know nothing about me, nothing at all!' the gipsy screamed in a last ditch effort to defend himself.

'Is that so?' Törner brought the exchange to an end, suggesting by his tone of voice that he knew more than he really did.

Then he stood up.

The sun was already up and shining through the curtains into the room. The turtledoves were cooing, the siskin singing. The baroness had fallen asleep on her chair and Ivan lay asleep between the two yellow dogs on the huge bed.

The gipsy wanted to pour more wine but Törner said no, after which his host followed him out into the kitchen.

A young girl was sitting there on the edge of the bed, half-dressed and pulling on her stockings. She stared at the stranger, so surprised that she forgot to cover herself.

'You should be ashamed of yourself, you slut!' the gipsy shouted, cuffing her around the head and throwing a blanket over her.

Andreas Törner said a hasty farewell and went up to his room to catch up on his sleep after the sleepless night.

*

Törner could not get a wink of sleep after that strange night in the baroness's apartments. He asked himself repeatedly how an individual as inferior as the gipsy could have such an effect on him that he filled his thoughts night and day. Could it result from that common law of attraction whereby the fluid in one body is drawn to that in another; which impels men to seek each other out; which leads to contact or rapport between individuals? Loneliness, the habit of meeting one and the same person several times a day, the adaptability that makes human intercourse possible, an interest in observing the secret processes of the soul – particularly a soul of such unusual character, occupying as it did the lowest rung of the ladder and thus of a kind a university professor only rarely had the opportunity to observe – all this meant that the gipsy had wormed his way into Törner's thoughts and lodged there, impossible to eject.

For his own peace of mind Törner had wanted to keep the relationship neutral but during that night their minds had momentarily come into collision, a spark had jumped from one to the other, their interests had intersected and there was conflict in the air. Törner, tired of his shabby role as admirer of this wretch, had demonstrated his superiority without pulling any punches, but he had been careless enough to hint that he had been thinking about the gipsy and his affairs. The gipsy, who had thought himself secure behind a palisade of lies, had recognized his error, sensed an observant eye being kept on him and a hand reaching into his very innards, and he had woken from his sense of security. Törner noticed this and, having no desire to waste time and energy on a meaningless struggle with such a low and unworthy individual, decided to lull him back into his earlier tranquillity and ensure that any unavoidable dealings between them were polite but lukewarm. Meanwhile he would keep himself to himself and shut his eyes to anything he could not avoid seeing and hearing.

With this in mind he went down to the garden on Sunday morning to take a walk. It was already the beginning of June but the ground had not been dug and any hope of planting anything was long past.

Calves, goats, sheep and horses were tethered to the trunks of the fruit trees and were grazing on the weeds. The goats, standing on their hind legs, were chewing the precious bushes and young fruit trees. The beasts had fouled the pathways and trampled down the boxwood hedges. The hens were eating the unripe currants and magpies and starlings were nesting in the cherry trees. It was a horrifying wasteland and Törner could not understand how these people, who were not short of financial resources, could bear to look at it. And even if they had no need of the income he thought they might still have enjoyed the pleasure of walking in the garden. The lush growth of weeds of dark and poisonous appearance served only to emphasize the impression of filth created by the animal droppings trampled into all the beds, by the small black molehills, by the rotting branches and last year's brown leaves.

Burdock and nettles, plants that always flourish where there is human excrement, were growing to a height of several feet, betraying what is normally kept concealed. Thistles, blown in from the fields, had found a home here. Coltsfoot, often jokingly called the horn of plenty because of its amazing ability to spread, grew in huge grey-green carpets and, in the darkest corners – like the deeds of darkness – vile henbane lurked, its corpse-yellow flower reminiscent of a cadaver with clotted blood. Master Törner, thinking of the danger this poisonous weed presented to his children, raised his stick and massacred it, at which he heard the lamenting voice of the gipsy behind a bush. He was not unduly surprised since he was now quite used to seeing the latter creeping in and out of bushes and hedges or, in fact, anywhere there was a place to hide.

'Don't beat down my henbane!' the gipsy bade him.

'Why? Is that sacred as well?' Törner answered, with a jocular reference to the death of the snake.

'No, it isn't, but I save the seed!'

'I see. What do you do with it?' Törner asked.

'It's good for all kinds of things,' the gipsy answered with a sly look that was meant to suggest he knew more than he was prepared to reveal.

Törner would later remember this incident with the henbane and feel it supported his earliest impressions that there was something suspicious about the inhabitants of the house and their doings.

This, however, was only the start of what the gipsy had to say. He immediately linked the henbane with something else that was on his mind.

'There is someone round here,' he began with a thoughtful expression, pouting his lips to suggest profundity and mystery as he always did when he was lying, 'there is someone round here who could do with a good dose of henbane.'

'What do you mean by that?' Törner exclaimed with the embarrassment of a man unfairly suspected or threatened. 'What's happened?'

'I'll tell you what's happened. What's happened is that someone has stolen one of the peacocks this morning,' the gipsy said with such emphasis that anyone guilty of the deed would undoubtedly have been conscience-stricken.

Andreas Törner smiled at the thought that he might be under suspicion but let himself to be drawn into discussing the matter even though it had nothing to do with him. The mysterious fact that a peacock had been stolen in broad daylight, right under the windows of the house and from an enclosed yard where people passed back and forth – all this, as Törner immediately pointed out, seemed unlikely. Meanwhile, the baroness, Ivan and the girl with tousled hair arrived wailing loudly and bemoaning the loss of the bird.

Suspicion was cast in all directions. The yard was inspected and a piece of the bird's long tail was discovered.

'It's the fox, of course,' the baroness assured them. 'He's forever pulling out the hens' tail-feathers.'

At first the gipsy pretended to go along with this view but nevertheless seemed uncertain what to think and so let the others do the talking. Törner thought it highly unlikely a fox would risk coming in daylight when it could have come at night since the peacocks slept out in the open.

The discussion went back and forth until eventually Törner and the gipsy were left alone together.

They examined the case from all possible angles and Törner stuck to the sensible view that only someone working in the house could have committed the theft. And when they went through the staff the suspicion fell naturally enough on the two carpenters, who were almost always out of sight. But once the conversation began to veer in that direction the gipsy performed a sudden *volte-face*.

No, there couldn't be any question of that: the carpenters were utterly honest, but there was someone who almost certainly was guilty – and that was the gatekeeper who lived in the nearby cottage.

Törner found it inconceivable that a stranger had climbed over the stone wall into the yard in broad daylight to steal the bird but did not want to complicate matters even more by disagreeing. He let the conversation die and went up to his room, feeling unpleasantly affected by the whole inexplicable business.

When he went down into the garden in the evening he met the

gipsy idling away his time. For lack of any other topic the conversation turned to the peacock. They were approaching the turkey coop where the cock had already gone inside and the hen was sitting on her eggs under a little pile of straw outside. Törner, not knowing what to talk about, suggested it would be impossible for anyone to catch a peacock with his bare hands.

'Oh, yes you can and I'll show you,' the gipsy answered, his urge to contradict wakened. 'If you can catch a turkey you can catch a peacock.'

In a flash he had his arms round the big ill-tempered turkey and was clutching it to him like a kitten. And to underline the likelihood of the gatekeeper being the thief he claimed to have seen people who could catch a pigeon on the ground. There were people who knew all kinds of tricks. He knew people – that's to say, he'd heard of people – who enticed other people's chickens and ducks away by laying down long trails of corn. Horse-traders were the most cunning of all: last year a red horse had been stolen from a neighbour – the farmer up at the crossroads – and no-one had seen a sign of it since. But he knew how they'd done it. They could change the colour of a horse by rubbing it with some kind of grease which made its hair fall out and when the new hair grew in it was never the same colour as the old. And you could give a horse a white blaze by making a few cuts with a knife since the hair always grew back white when the cuts healed.

All these things were new and unfamiliar to Törner and in his eagerness to hear them he omitted to ask where the factor had acquired such knowledge. So they walked on, becoming engrossed in a conversation that seemed to be of profound interest to the gipsy. They moved on to theft in general and the gipsy voiced his scorn for most thieves since, as a rule, they fail to understand the two essential points about all thieving.

'And what are they?' Törner asked as innocently as possible after they had sat down on a stone bench at the edge of the lake.

'Well, it's like this...' the gipsy pondered for a moment, 'the first thing is never to have any accomplices and the second is to have two people to back up your story.'

'To give you an *alibi*, is that it? You know what that means?'

The gipsy looked thoughtful for a couple of seconds, seeming to have no idea what the word *alibi* meant but, as ever, he did not want to reveal his ignorance and so he answered:

'You tell me what you mean by it first and... mmh... I'll tell you afterwards what I think.'

'An *alibi*,' Törner began, 'is the most important aspect of any defence case since if I can prove that at that particular time I was somewhere other than the scene of the crime I will be acquitted.'

'Exactly what I was going to say,' the gipsy broke in with unfeigned pleasure on his pale face. 'But,' he continued, 'being alone is still the first rule of thieving.'

'Yes, that's probably true,' Master Törner agreed, 'but even more important is to be sure not to leave any kind of *corpus delicti*. Do you know what a *corpus delicti* is?'

Well, he thought he had a pretty good idea what it was but couldn't put it into words properly, so he'd like to hear Törner's opinion first and then he'd say whether he thought the same thing.

Törner, who had recently been studying law, answered: 'A *corpus delicti* may be an object found in the possession of the apprehended, or it may be an object which a felon has left behind at the scene of the crime or, in the case of murder, it may be a weapon, for example. Is that what you thought?'

'Yes, more or less,' the gipsy answered quickly with a long face.

'Moreover,' Törner continued, imagining he was standing at the lectern – a temptation he frequently fell into – 'moreover, the person apprehended would be well-advised to agree to all the details but to deny the main accusation. A murderer should admit that he was present at the scene of the murder in case someone has seen him there but he should always put it in such a way that, with a semblance of truth, he can claim to have been there for some other purpose. It is foolish to deny everything. That way you simply get entangled in contradictions. And the worst thing of all is to lose control of your tongue and start firing off threats and demands: that way, however innocent you may be, you are risking your neck for something you didn't do. You are a careless fellow,

Jensen. The other day you were openly wishing that lightning would strike the stable so you could claim the fire insurance and build a new one. Now, what if the stable had burnt down last night? Even though you weren't necessarily the guilty party I would have suspected you simply because you'd expressed a desire for it to happen and you would have profited from it happening.'

'Would you report me?' the gipsy asked quickly.

Master Törner had to think carefully before answering.

'It's like this,' he said when he finally spoke, 'there are what we might call suggestions and what we can call accusations. What I mean by suggestions is that I may have my suspicions and pass them on privately to the authorities with the idea that they carry out their own independent investigation; and it's only on the basis of the latter that they come to any decision about making an arrest. But there are so many antiquated features and inefficient procedures in our legal system that I'd like to see a good deal of it changed... Tell me something: are you intending to report the gatekeeper as a possible suspect for the theft of the bird?'

The gipsy answered quickly:

'No, I can't risk it since he's well in with the authorities.'

'Well, you should see to it that you are too,' Törner answered, wishing to give the gipsy a gentle reminder. 'And I don't understand why you hate someone who protects your property and without whom you wouldn't get a sound night's sleep.'

The gipsy broke into a string of oaths aimed at the gatekeeper, claiming he was the worst kind of rogue imaginable. He worked himself up to such a pitch that he finally blurted out that he would like to see him lying by the ditch with his throat cut. Then he suddenly checked himself and brought the conversation back to crimes and criminals in general. Master Törner, for whom hitherto unsuspected horizons were being opened and who had wondered why the gipsy – given his suspicions – did not bring charges against the gatekeeper, decided to try to discover the hidden reason that was preventing the gipsy taking action against his neighbour. So he adopted his lecturing tone once more, as if continuing his discourse on the practice and administration of law from a purely philosophical standpoint.

'One very common practice among dyed-in-the-wool criminals is to implicate the person who would be the most dangerous witness.'

'What does implicate mean?' the gipsy asked eagerly.

'There are many ways of implicating someone. One way is to let the witness see as much as possible of the preparations for the crime so that, when the perpetrator is arrested, it can be claimed that the witness was fully cognizant of the crime but remained silent. It is important, however, in such a situation not to let him see so much that there's a risk of him warning the authorities in advance. Do you understand his dilemma, the trap that's been set for him? Whether the witness notifies the authorities or not, he will be involved in the case – that is, he will be implicated.'

'That's magnificent!' the gipsy exclaimed excitedly. 'That's magnificent!' And his face shone with delight.

'Another method frequently used by criminals of some sophistication is to attempt to establish in advance grounds that will disqualify the witness. Do you know what disqualification is? It might include some kind of blood relationship or even a betrothal or some loose connection with the accused. It could even be the fact that the witness is known to be an enemy of or envious of the accused. Thus, if anyone could prove your carpenters were the gatekeeper's enemies, they would be disqualified as witnesses against him.'

'Is that really true?' the gipsy exclaimed and tried to take Törner by the hand. 'You must have read and studied a huge number of books to have all that at your fingertips!'

He at once regretted this excessive show of enthusiasm and the demon of arrogance came to the surface again.

'I should add by the way that I've read loads of books too,' he informed Törner. 'I don't suppose you've read the book about the Count of Luxembourg?'

'No, I haven't,' Törner answered truthfully. 'But I've heard of him and I've heard you sing the song about him.'

'Oh, that's some book that, believe me!' the gipsy said,

58

assuming an air of importance in view of Törner's ignorance. 'It's a book everyone can learn something from. And it's enjoyable. Just think about it: a count who steals and murders and the police can never catch him however hard they try. He was a crafty fellow, I can tell you. He used to visit the graves of criminals in churchyards in order to poison nails that he would then hammer into the chairs of people he wanted to dispose of. Corpses are poisonous, you know. And he never stole anything but money since money is impossible to identify and can be used again without worrying. He never stole treasure and jewellery. So when the police came searching there was nothing to find.'

He had been talking enthusiastically but now he came to a sudden stop as though worried he had said too much.

And to conceal his mistake he turned angrily towards the gatekeeper's cottage, which could be glimpsed through the bushes, clenched his fist and exclaimed:

'Oh yes, there are so many crooks in the world! That gatekeeper – now he's a really nasty piece of work!'

Törner felt some disquiet after this conversation and, half regretting what he had said in the course of the evening, went to bed with a troubled mind.

*

A week later Master Andreas Törner was taking his regular morning walk. His mood was depressed, the past week having been filled with events that would have disturbed the balance of mind of any man, however calm his disposition. Walking through the woods the day after the conversation about crimes and criminals Törner had found several blue breast feathers from the stolen peacock and taken them home with him. He had shown his finds, thinking that by doing so he would clear the gatekeeper of suspicion since they effectively proved that a fox was the guilty party. His statements were greeted with disbelief and the gipsy objected that really experienced criminals know how to divert attention from themselves by providing a false '*corpus delictum*'.

So now Törner was being paid back for all his learning. *Corpus delictum*, indeed!

The next morning Törner had found some of the bird's quill feathers – cut cleanly with a knife this time. When he brought these home the gipsy was triumphant: surely he didn't imagine the fox went round with a knife in its pocket?

The following night the turkey cock was stolen and there was no trace of it anywhere.

The next evening Törner and the gipsy were standing by the iron gate when the son of the district judge, a landowner in his own right, came riding along, stopped his horse and asked in a rather peremptory manner whether he could buy the drake that was waddling around on the grass. The gipsy answered politely that he would not sell it.

During the night the drake disappeared.

A number of circumstances made the events difficult to explain. If the fox had taken the turkey cock, which had been sitting on its perch in its coop and was strong enough to defend itself, why had it not taken the hen which was sitting on its eggs on straw out in the open – all the more so as those with knowledge of such things said that a fox would not tackle a turkey cock but could certainly manage the hen.

And why was the drake stolen during the night that followed a visit by the judge's son? It would be crazy to suspect a rich and respectable man and no-one on the estate dared suggest any such thing. Was there something behind all this or was it just a coincidence? And what about the carefully cut feathers, which had quite clearly been placed with a view to Törner discovering them? What was the point of that? If the gatekeeper was the thief, surely he would not go and lay out evidence that proved the fox to be innocent? Nor would the carpenters have done so if they were guilty. So, who had put out the feathers, and why? One riddle after another!

On top of all this the sheriff and later his deputy had come to Bögely to inspect the scene of the thefts. The sheriff had been given a hearty welcome by the baroness and the gipsy, who had served him wine and sent for Törner, whom they described as an enthusiastic friend of the Danes. They had gone on to heap praise on Törner and boast about him, as if they wanted to scrape some of the gold off him and gild themselves with it. The gipsy had even portrayed him as his good and intimate friend, his teacher, his confidant; so much so that it upset Törner and he tried to reject this flattery without, as far as possible, giving offence. The most remarkable thing about the whole business was that exactly the same performance was laid on when the deputy visited a little later.

After that the gatekeeper was quickly hauled up in front of the magistrate in Hälsingborg – not, however, for the theft of the birds but for stealing some planks; but just as they were about to lock up the gatekeeper, the gipsy – as plaintiff – suddenly decided to be magnanimous and not to press charges. At which the tearful gatekeeper thanked his benefactor and even the magistrate praised him for his generous behaviour.

The day before the two parties went to court, the carpenters had disappeared and been replaced by two new ones, who were given express orders not to set foot in the gatekeeper's house since he ran an illicit tavern there.

Events followed each other in such rapid succession that Törner was unable to keep up with them or work out any meaning or connection. Least of all could he make sense of a subsequent event that came as more of a surprise than all the others together. One morning he found the tousle-haired girl in his bedroom making his bed and when he questioned his wife she said that, since help was needed round the house, she had taken on the girl as housemaid on the recommendation of the factor. What is more, the carpenters claimed the girl was the gipsy's sister, although he refused to admit the fact and she, like Ivan, had to address her brother as *monsieur*.

So, as Master Törner continued his walk through the beech wood and came to a plantation where a path overhung by young spruce trees led up the hill on which he had found the peacock feathers, he began to put his impressions in order. His main conclusion was that strange things were going on in the house: a net was being spun round him and he himself, without knowing it, had perhaps provided the threads.

He was quite unable to fathom the purpose of all this since the gipsy twisted and turned and laid false trails like a hare in the snow and Törner was unable to track all the whims of his confused brain. When he put all his suspicions on one side of the scales, however, he could only think of one counterweight: the fact that the gipsy's sound financial state must surely free him from any temptation to be a thief.

The relationship between Törner and the gipsy had been a good one in recent days, friendlier and more ingratiating, however, on the part of the latter than of the former. The old self-confident tone the gipsy had used during their early times together had returned now that Törner no longer pressed uninvited learning on him, whether about music, agriculture or magic.

The baroness was staying out of sight and the singing and music downstairs had stopped, from which Törner concluded that the gipsy's performances as an artist no longer made any impression on his mistress. He also came to the conclusion, less than pleasant to contemplate, that the gipsy bore a grudge against him ever since that evening when the baroness hushed the gipsy's singing because Törner outshone the charlatan.

The sun shone down on the woodland path between the young spruce trees and as he walked Törner noticed the outline of fresh footprints in the fallen needles and he was certain he had not made them. A magpie flew up from the dense foliage and disappeared shrieking above the treetops. Törner came to a sudden halt, stared into the gloom and caught sight of a nest sitting between the branches and trunk of a young spruce. A cluster of sunbeams broke through, casting a greenish-yellow light on the trunks. Suddenly his attention was caught by a tree, on the bark of which various signs had been carved so deeply with a sharp knife that the white of the wood shone through and the resin ran in drips and streaks right to the foot of the tree.

Törner looked at the markings. They stood out clearly, revealing the sure workmanship of a practised hand, and the first thing that struck him was how similar they were to the Red Indian signs he had seen reproduced in a travel narrative from the New Sweden settlement on the Delaware river. He did not assume any direct connection between the two scripts as he knew enough to realize that hieroglyphs or sign languages are similar among all peoples. Since he could see a hand, a key and an eye depicted here, he concluded that by a combination of comparison and analysis it should be possible to decipher the meaning of these signs and thus get on the track of secrets that possibly concerned him more than he liked to think. He took out his note book and copied the signs as carefully as he could. But then, instead of turning for home, he continued along the path all the way to the gate and walked on to the boundaries of the estate with the intention of visiting his neighbours in order to learn more about the people from whom he was renting accommodation and who seemed to have secret plans to involve him in their affairs.

Half an hour later he entered Farmer Virup's porch and was met by a servant girl whom he asked to announce his visit. He was, however, quite determined to say nothing bad about his landlord nor to cast any suspicion on him.

When he went into the living room he saw Virup sitting on a bench by the stove studying him with sharp grey eyes. The farmer remained sitting but excused himself by saying he had gout in his legs.

Törner had no doubt what the gout implied: it was merely a cloak for lack of courtesy. Without further ado he therefore sat down in the best armchair and kept his hat on, excusing himself by saying he had a headache.

Then he stated his business.

'I've come,' he announced, 'to pay my respects to you as a neighbour and to ask a favour. You probably know who I am but certainly don't know what my function is in this part of the country. I'm a plant collector among other things and to carry out my studies I sometimes need to climb over the fences into other people's fields. May I have your permission to enter your fields if I promise not to trample down the corn?'

The farmer immediately gave his permission, unaccustomed to such courtesy on the part of his enemies. He even mellowed to the extent of making an effort to continue a conversation which had initially seemed less than attractive to him.

'Well,' he went on, 'so you're living at Bögely. What do you think of your landlord?'

This was just the question Törner had been hoping for and he was quick to take the opening.

'He's a sharp fellow, as far as I can judge.'

'A bit dodgy, though, isn't he?' the farmer sniggered.

'Not that I'd noticed,' Törner answered.

'He's getting through the baroness's money and property.'

'Do you really think so?' Törner asked, hoping to get at the truth by contradicting him. 'He's just an unpaid factor who walks behind the plough, mows the hay and waters the beasts like an ordinary labourer, so it seems to me that he earns his daily bread.'

'Well, I know you're very friendly with him,' the farmer answered, 'so I won't say anything bad about him!'

This worried Törner. Friendly with him! But he thought it was still too early to withdraw.

'Friendly? What do you mean by that? Friendship can only exist between people on the same cultural level,' he said, quoting Cicero's *De amicitia*, 'and I haven't yet done the factor the honour of taking him into my confidence.'

'I see, I see,' the farmer answered with a thoughtful look. 'I only know what people say, of course. And round here he's reckoned to be the worst kind of thieving rogue and, believe me, it'll be a miracle if the baroness doesn't end up in the workhouse before Michaelmas.'

'Really? Is that so?' Törner exclaimed. 'I understood the baroness was well-off.'

'She certainly used to be pretty well-off but that fellow's squandered it. Things have got to the point where her property is being distrained for taxes and highway dues. But he's a cunning one and when the sheriff comes to take the cattle he'll find they've been put in Jensen's name, as his property.'

This provided Törner with confirmation of the most important elements underlying the structure of suspicion he had built up. Now he understood why the estate was being allowed to fall into disrepair, why they cooked and ate food that was already rotting, why... Here he stopped and, to avoid the temptation of thinking aloud, desisted from further questioning, got to his feet, thanked the farmer for his kindness and bade him farewell.

The farmer, surprised at this abrupt conclusion to the conversation, forgot his gout and rose to accompany his guest to the door.

At the door it occurred to Törner that he should speak up and firmly repudiate any rumour that he was a friend of the gipsy's, something people could easily assume if he simply brushed aside information which had presumably been offered with the best of neighbourly intentions. But he hesitated and the expression on the farmer's face was so frosty that he could not bring himself to say anything, so he raised his hat and departed.

As he went out through the gate to walk home across the meadow he had the feeling he had made a blunder. But it was too late to turn back, particularly as he could see the gipsy standing guard close by the fence round the garden. There could be no doubt he had already noticed Törner.

Törner had no desire for a meeting with Jensen at the very moment he was coming away from a neighbour who had been voicing warnings about him. There was, however, no way of avoiding it and the only thing to do was to walk straight up to his adversary.

Jensen was walking along with his head bent and with a pole in his hand, pretending to measure the ground and showing no sign that he was aware of Törner's approach.

The latter said good morning in a loud voice. The gipsy feigned surprise but said nothing, for which reason Törner decided to tackle the subject head-on and say everything there was to say but without revealing the truth too clearly.

'I've been over to our neighbour's to ask permission to go on his land,' he explained.

The gipsy said nothing but forced a smile which tried to be friendly at the same time as demonstrating indifference to the whole business.

There was, however, no going back and Törner had to continue even if it led him into difficult waters, which it certainly did because he suddenly felt an irresistible urge to clear his conscience.

'You don't have any friends in the district, Jensen,' he said. 'The farmer over the way has nothing good to say of you.'

'I can believe that!' the gipsy answered. 'There was a time when he was after the baroness and her money and when nothing came of it I was the one he poured the dirt over.'

Master Törner, who was used to the gipsy wiping his own dirt off on others, took this to be a lie but pretended to believe the accusation.

'That's what I said to him,' he continued, 'and I said more than that, because I could hear that he was jealous. I praised you, Jensen, as an energetic and unselfish fellow who gets out and works in the fields even though you are the factor – something which no other factor in the country would do. And I suggested that the baroness could hardly feel any great affection for you since she lets you slave away without wages.'

Finding it impossible to believe that Törner might be lying when he had never done so before, the gipsy swallowed this. Pleased to have convinced Törner of his honesty, he grasped his hand and pressed it with genuine emotion, thanking the lucky star which had led him at last to an honourable man who spoke well of him. He surrendered to his emotions, opened his heart and talked of the recent bad harvests that had ruined them, of the evil people who had tricked them out of the money they had lent them, of the burden of providing food for the animals and the people every week, of anything and everything that could rouse sympathy for himself and his situation.

While the gipsy was in this emotional frame of mind and apparently ready to listen to good advice, Master Törner took the opportunity to remonstrate with him on the foolishness of not cultivating the fields, which would at least provide bread. He tried to convince him that it would be better housekeeping to hire people to work the land than for him, as factor, to waste his own time doing it.

'If you lie on a bench, smoke your pipe and keep an eye on the workers, it will be much more valuable than if you, as a townsman with refined habits, toil in the fields,' he concluded his lecture.

The idea of lying on a bench smoking his pipe seemed to appeal to the gipsy and he admitted for the first time that Törner was a wise man, full of good advice, of which he would be happy to take advantage.

When Master Andreas Törner parted from his grateful disciple he felt full of the kind of sympathy one feels for an unfortunate and self-pitying wretch – and of the calm satisfaction that came from knowing that the gipsy was now under an obligation to him. After this outburst he felt safer, no longer afraid of the gipsy, and all his rancour about small injustices and insolence disappeared along with his fear. He forgot all his suspicions even though they had recently been confirmed by the information he had received about the man's economic situation.

As he walked through the garden in this noble frame of mind he caught sight of a figure lying prostrate on the ground at the foot of the sun dial. It was, as he soon discovered, the tousle-haired servant girl.

'Why are you lying here, Magelone?' he asked, surprised to see her outside at a time of the day when she was usually cleaning his room.

The girl got up slowly and, hiding her red eyes and tear-streaked cheeks with her hand, she sniffled:

'Mistress has thrown me out!'

'Why, child?' Törner asked.

The girl was silent for a moment and then managed to sniff:

'Mistress said I wasn't smart enough and I've only got one dress and I wear it all the time. But I can't help that.'

He looked at the tousled girl who, although filthy, was dolled out in two pearl necklaces and earrings and he immediately saw the truth of the matter though he did not have the heart to tell her. So he bade her not to be upset with her mistress, who was very ill and who had certainly not meant her any harm.

The servant girl looked at him through spread fingers and asked in the most pleading voice she was capable of:

'You'll take me back, won't you Master?'

'Well, my child, these are things I don't get involved in. It's my wife's job to deal with it!' he answered and went on his way, depressed by this attempt to use him to settle a quarrel he knew nothing about.

When he reached the front steps his children's nursemaid was outside beating the bedclothes.

'What's all this about Magelone?' he asked.

'She's a fine one, that one,' the nursemaid answered. 'She's only gone and brought bugs into the beds and given the children a rash. Mistress has forbidden her to kiss them but she still does it. And when she got sacked she spat like a cat and cursed and swore that all you Swedish riff-raff would pay for it!'

While the nursemaid was giving vent to her vexation Master Törner noticed something moving behind a curtain on the floor where the baroness lived. He realized someone was listening.

'It's a tedious business,' he said to himself as he went up to his room, his mind troubled by forebodings brought on by what he knew of gipsies' implacable desire for vengeance for any injury inflicted on them. But then he remembered the friendly conversation he had just had with her brother Jensen; and his thoughts ranged back to his morning visit to the neighbouring farmer and the information he had got there; and he remembered the mysterious inscriptions he had seen. All the dark and unpleasant events that had occurred in this house passed before his eyes and he was seized by a powerful desire to be out of it all. He decided to leave everything and travel away, it did not matter where, as soon as possible.

There were things happening here, he felt – intrigues that were beginning to enmesh him and might end by choking him.

Part II

New and unexpected things happened on the estate in the course of the week Master Andreas Törner was waiting for a reply to his application for permission to leave the district.

A farm-labourer and a gardener arrived. The labourer, who soon realized the factor knew nothing about farmwork, took to lazing around and began a love affair with the girl with the tousled hair. And the gardener, who knew it was too late to do any digging, saw no point in starting any real work anyway since he was not getting an assistant; so he spent most of his time sitting in the cherry trees picking cherries that had already started to rot on the branches.

The gipsy himself lay on a bench and smoked his pipe, faithfully following Törner's improvised advice and, when he was not sleeping or smoking, he was drinking or out riding the horse, mostly at night. His attitude towards Master Törner was one of arrogant superiority and he expounded grandiose plans for the improvement of the estate and even grander ideas for the expansion of the garden. He said nothing about his sister's dismissal from her post but there seemed to be a wild glint in his eyes whenever he met Törner's children or servants, and the latter had to be on their guard against the dogs, which Ivan and Magelone surreptitiously set on them from any available hiding place. The Törners no longer dared allow their children to roam free in the garden and they were kept in the house except when the nursemaid was free to walk with them.

When Törner informed him of his intention to move, the gipsy was too impatient to listen to the end and immediately showed his true nature by grinning maliciously and referring to the contract.

Master Törner quickly replied that the contract could not compel him to continue living there, only to pay the rent until the closing date in October.

Once notice had been given, the relationship between them might have become even more strained, but the gipsy's admiration for Törner actually grew when he saw that he was not trying to evade his contractual responsibility. Törner seemed prepared to be cheated without protest.

Törner's desire to leave grew even stronger after he made what struck him as a disquieting discovery. In spite of repeated reminders over the months he had still not been provided with a lock for the door of his room, which consequently remained unlocked day and night. One afternoon he could see that someone had been in there and moved his books while he was out. He noticed that his dissertation on the science of assaying was upside down and bore the marks of dirty fingers. Clearly the gipsy had been in: instead of asking permission to borrow books, which would not have been refused, his thieving nature had led him to sneak in and read them. Master Törner angrily summoned a locksmith and then sent him down to the baroness for payment, which he duly received. But when he mentioned in passing what he had done, the gipsy was unable to contain his annoyance and embarrassment since he realized he had been discovered.

The atmosphere was now so charged that an explosion seemed likely at any moment though, since parting was imminent, both sides tried to avoid the outbreak of hostilities. Törner's longing for the moment of departure increased further following two more events that he found thoroughly unpleasant even though he was now familiar with the disastrous state of the establishment. One morning when he went into the garden he saw the two carpenters hastily hammering together a dung-cart, which was shaped like a coffin with a sloping lid. Just for something to say, Master Törner jokingly asked:

'What are you going to use that coffin for?'

One of the carpenters was quick to reply and he too adopted a jocular tone:

'Well, it won't be the first time corpses have been carried in a thing like this.'

'What do you mean by that?' Törner asked, perceiving an element of seriousness in the answer.

'Actually, all I'm saying is that dung-carts are where the corpses of infants are usually found. My father was a prison warder, you see, so I heard all kinds of things.'

The gipsy, who was standing beside them in silence, was looking down at the ground. Then he looked up and cut short the unpleasant conversation.

'We're putting the garden in order so I've made an arrangement with the cavalry stables in Landskrona to go there to fetch manure.'

Törner would have paid no attention to this trivial matter if, as he continued his walk through the garden, he had not met the gardener down by the hothouse.

'Are you really going to spread dung during the summer?' he asked him, without any real interest in the answer.

'Well, it's certainly not something I've done before. But the factor says he's made a firm agreement with the royal stockyard in Hälsingborg and he doesn't want to wait.'

'What did you say?' Törner began but immediately stopped himself, determined not to say anything that might reveal the gipsy's mendacity.

The following night, by which time the cart was finished, Master Törner was wakened by noises up in the attic rooms. He got up and listened carefully in case he had been mistaken but was soon convinced there were people upstairs doing something they were trying to conceal – they were unlikely to be bothering to move stealthily out of consideration for those sleeping below. It sounded as if they were dragging a heavy object which was bumping into the various things piled up there.

The thought of thieves did not enter Törner's mind since the dogs had been unchained and sniffing around the whole estate all evening and the gipsy had warned off any nocturnal wanderers in the locality by going round the house firing off his pistol.

Since he was sure he was dealing with the residents of the house Törner wanted to find out whether or not they were trying to keep their actions secret. In order not to surprise them and possibly push them into taking dangerous defensive measures, he rose from his bed and asked through the door whether there was anyone there. Everything immediately went quiet, so he said, as if talking to himself but loud enough for the people in the attic to hear and assume they had fooled him: 'I must have been dreaming.'

Then he went back to bed, pretended to fall asleep and snored loudly.

After a while the noises in the attic resumed and he heard footsteps creeping away down the stairs.

Törner's thoughts ran in all directions but always returned to the dung-cart which, for no apparent reason, had been constructed in such haste. His thoughts also turned to the fourth tower room, into which he had never looked and where the gipsy claimed to have his quarters. He recalled the mendacious and contradictory accounts of where the manure was to be collected; and finally he wondered why the dogs had been unchained the evening before.

With his imagination over-excited by lack of sleep, Törner's fevered mind filled with old tales of heirs who had been incarcerated in attics and starved to death. Stories of robberies and smuggling, both old and new, surfaced in his memory but he rejected them as quickly as they came. He thought of opening the window and continuing his investigation but did not want to risk revealing himself as a spy.

So he turned to the wall and soon fell asleep. When he woke the sun was already high in the sky.

The events of the night stood out sharp and vivid and he realized that it was impossible to behave as if nothing had happened since silence was more likely to arouse suspicion than speech. Thus, when he came down and met the baroness, he greeted her genially and asked whether she too had heard noises in the attic during the night.

No, she had heard nothing.

'Oh, I was so frightened,' Törner said, assuming his most innocent expression, 'I thought we had thieves.'

'No, surely not, how could you think such a thing? How could they possibly have got in?' the baroness asked with feigned alarm.

'They could have climbed in from the cherry tree.'

'No, I can't believe it. It must have been the cats,' the baroness said. 'I did leave the attic door open yesterday evening. There are so many rats and they gnaw everything we store up there.'

Not wishing to pursue the matter further Master Törner pretended to believe the story about the cats, even adding reasons of his own in support of that explanation. He was now utterly convinced that they wanted to conceal their nocturnal activities.

But, his rational mind reminded him, the fact that people want to hide things from outsiders does not necessarily imply criminal intent. People hide their business affairs and they hide their poverty, their family secrets and their sorrows so why, in this particular case, should he suspect criminal activities?

When he went down to the garden the dung-cart was gone and the gardener told him that the factor had gone to Denmark to buy chickens.

He did not want to ask any more questions, but one thing was certain: the dung-cart was gone and it had certainly not gone to Denmark. Was it also untrue that the gipsy had gone to Denmark?

A little while later they brought out the great coach and harnessed the horses, and the baroness, Ivan and Magelone set off to visit Landskrona in order, so they said, to watch an animal trainer perform, it being Magelone's birthday.

They set off and returned at nightfall so tired or drunk that they slept in the carriage until broad daylight when Master Törner came down to find the strange trio still snoring with the sun shining straight in their faces. The baroness was the first to come to, heard the cows mooing and remembered that they had not been milked for the last twenty-four hours. At which she looped up her cape and sat down to milk them in all her finery.

Meanwhile Magelone had woken up. Rubbing the sleep from her eyes, she approached Törner with a peculiar secretive expression and began to speak, stammering, her eyes unsteady and her physical movements confused.

'Can you believe it, Sir? We found the peacock at the animal trainer's.'

'No, but that's impossible!'

'No it isn't! And it recognized the baroness straightaway and came up to her to be fed. And the baroness held it.'

'Yes, dear girl, but how could you recognize it?' Törner asked, still believing her story.

'Because it didn't have any tail feathers. And, anyway, the baroness knew her own bird. But you mustn't tell Jensen, Sir,' she added.

The baroness called her and that was the end of the conversation.

Törner's mind began to work and he asked himself: *pro primo*, how could the bird be there when its breast feathers with skin attached had been found out in the woods? *Pro secundo*, why should Jensen not be told about it?

Was all this just one more in the series of lies they had cobbled together? Or did they really believe that the bird was there – and did the girl suspect her own brother of having stolen it?

The way these people thought ran in such serpentine coils that it was hard to follow them. And with his moment of liberation approaching Törner had no desire to bother clearing up things that were of no concern to him. But the thoughts would not go away: they demanded an answer and the fact that his mind was being forced into involvement with the petty affairs of petty people filled him with rage. Whoever it was who had stolen the bird, it had nothing to do with him; whatever the explanation for it may or may not be was of no consequence to him; yet he was wasting mental energy attempting to achieve clarity. Three whole months, a quarter of a year, isolated from intercourse with people of culture and confined in the company of creatures of a lower order, had changed him without him even being aware of it. His thoughts, which had previously been taken up with the higher questions of life, which had tried to penetrate the mysteries of existence and the universe, were now occupied with trivialities and the construction of syllogisms to work out who had stolen a bird. Other people's petty concerns had insinuated themselves into his soul and he could not hear a cow moo without wondering whether they had forgotten to milk it, could not look at a neglected field without making plans to weed it. If he heard the gipsy leave, he wondered where he was going; if he saw the carpenters start a job, he asked himself what the purpose was; if the gipsy uttered a word, however unimportant, he analyzed it carefully to see what lay behind it or how far from the truth it was.

When he examined himself, he found he had adopted a number of the gipsy's gestures, borrowed certain tones of voice and, even worse, mixed Danish words and expressions into his speech. He had been jabbering with these infantile people for so long that he was forgetting how to speak properly; he had been lowering himself to their level for so long that his back was becoming hunched; he had been hearing lies for so long that he had come to believe that everyone lied. And he, a strong man who had never been afraid of battle, noticed that his courage was beginning to desert him, that cowardice and fear were creeping up on him in this struggle against invisible powers and enemies who were superior because they did not shrink from using weapons he could not bring himself to employ.

And the girl's story came back to him, unsheathed its claws and slashed and tore at his mind.

Was she lying? Of course she was! No animal trainer was going to buy a peacock without a tail and with its feathers torn out. And peacocks do not moult their tails until autumn.

Why was she lying? Was she trying to convince Törner that the gatekeeper was guilty, or what was it?

And why should he not tell Jensen? Perhaps she really meant him to tell Jensen? On the basis of her own low moral nature she had possibly concluded that the surest way of encouraging him to tell Jensen was to ask him to keep it secret? Did she think the temptation to tell tales was increased by forbidding it? It was impossible for him to discover any meaning or clarity in all this and so it possessed him like an incubus.

The gipsy came home with the cart that evening, bringing a large coop containing seventy-five chickens. Master Törner was standing in the garden when he arrived and he soon elicited a long account of the journey. Twenty-five chickens had escaped on the ferry from Elsinore to Hälsingborg and flown into the sea but even though this was an appreciable loss the gipsy did not seem in the least put out. Having claimed to be ruined he had proceeded to behave like a rich man for whom no sum of money was too great. He even inveigled Ivan into lying to Törner's maidservant about an enormous win on the Amsterdam lottery.

With the arrival of the chickens the labourers gathered around the coop. The gipsy left them for a moment and Törner, sympathizing with the loss, began to examine the hole through which the birds were supposed to have flown out. One of the carpenters immediately gave a grunt of disbelief and could not resist saying in a low voice:

'I bet those birds flew into his own pocket!'

So even his own workmen suspected the gipsy of stealing from the baroness.

It was not unreasonable, then, to assume that he had also stolen the other birds. Could he really be such a shameless wretch as to let innocent people take the blame?

Törner's disgust was so overwhelming that he had to leave the estate. He set off down along the main highway where it was clean and dry and, since it was evening and the mounted post was expected at any moment, he decided to walk to meet him. The road ran straight as an arrow between willow trees towards the high ground around Lund and Törner could pick out a rider several miles away coming in the direction of Bögely. Sometimes, when the rider was in a hollow, only his head and shoulders could be seen, sometimes the whole figure was visible on his heavy horse. The evening sun shone directly on the rider and Törner wondered why he could not see the gleam of his helmet. But after a short while he saw that the horseman was only wearing a hat and so could not be the post-rider. After waiting so long in vain Törner turned for home in a bad humour. He was indifferent to the approaching hoof beats and the voice calling him from behind.

'Hello there, old friend!' came the sound of a powerful voice while the horse gave him a friendly nudge with its nose.

'Bureus! It can't really be you, can it?' Törner exclaimed and grasped his friend's hand, overcome with joy at seeing a soul mate; and like a shipwrecked sailor meeting people ashore or a lost dog reunited with its master he deluged his visitor with exclamations of joy, uttering a stream of disconnected words and coming close to choking on his sobs.

'I hope you're bringing me good news from the *Consistorium academicum*,' he said at last, having recovered his composure somewhat.

'Unfortunately not, my dear friend!' Professor Bureus answered and handed him a letter. 'Quite the opposite. I'm here to inspect you and to get your report on the behaviour of the population in your district.'

Master Andreas Törner stood there with his head bowed as if someone had struck him. Then he straightened up, took the horse by the bridle and led it in through the gate while all the dogs on the estate ran at them, for which they received an angry kicking from the enraged Törner.

Since his children and sick wife had already gone to bed, he invited his friend to join him for supper down in the summerhouse, where they lit lanterns and sat down to talk while they waited for the food.

In a long and uninterrupted torrent Törner poured out an account of his sufferings, vexations and anxieties but when he began to give a detailed explanation of his suspicions his friend broke in:

'You're ill, Andreas.'

'Me?' Törner exclaimed in amazement.

'Yes! Loneliness and bad company have made you confused while fear of the unknown has sapped all your strength. You're living with a gang of thieves, that's all there's to it.'

'Do you think so? Do you really think so? Well, thank God for that – in that case I'm not afraid any more. What I was most frightened of was that I was suffering from some kind of sick delusion that was leading me to be unjust to innocent people. Well, God be praised. Now, you've studied philology, haven't you? Can you tell me what these symbols mean? I found them carved on a tree in the woods.'

He took out his notebook and showed his friend the signs he had copied down.

Bureus cast his eye quickly over the drawing.

'It's very strange,' he said, 'how individuals of low standing, whichever nation they may belong to, come up with exactly the same inventions. If this hand or this eye or this key had been drawn by a West Indian or an Egyptian or a Chinaman they would have been just as easy for me to interpret. The hand is being used here as a verb and means "to take"; the key probably means "to unlock" and, since we are talking about thieves in this case, "to open other people's locks"; and then the eye – that no doubt just means "to see". Hang on a minute...'

The professor put his hand over his eyes while he concentrated on finding a meaningful combination of the three signs and after a few minutes' pause he explained:

'This is what it means: the theft has been carried out but someone is keeping an eye on us. In other words, they suspect you! Now, do you know what you should do to give them a false sense of security – and then to frighten them?'

Master Törner answered no and waited expectantly for more.

'Right, I suggest you go to the woods and carve, let's say, an arrow through the eye. Even if that doesn't exactly match the thieves' language they will take it to mean that the eye has been blinded – which they'll interpret as meaning that you can no longer see anything, that you've been fooled. Then you'll be free to spy on them until it's time to fetch the constable and throw the whole gang into gaol.'

The professor had just finished speaking when the maids came in with supper and set it on the table. Behind them appeared the gipsy, dressed in his yellow jacket and the fancy hat with the peacock feather. For whatever reason, he seemed to have dressed up for the evening and he staggered as he approached the table. Without raising his hat he greeted the professor in a familiar manner and the latter found it impossible to refrain from laughing. The gipsy was so drunk his eyes were rolling in their sockets. He supported himself with one hand on the table, crossed his legs and started talking in a tone that suggested he had been invited to join them.

'Nice weather this evening,' he began.

'Please help yourself,' Törner interrupted, inviting Bureus to partake of the food while pretending not to notice the gipsy, whose eyes were flashing.

The two gentlemen began to eat even though the uninvited guest showed no sign of leaving them.

'Your good health, old friend! Welcome!' Törner said and poured him beer from the jug.

'Your good health, colleague!' the professor answered.

The gipsy slunk back to the wall like a hunted lynx but had still not given up hope of being invited.

'Have you come far, Sir?' he said, trying to force himself on them again.

'Keep your mouth shut, you, and go to hell!' the professor snapped in fury, but then decided to have some fun and kicked the gipsy's crossed legs into the air so that he sat down on the summerhouse floor banging his head on a stone.

Törner, fearing the gypsy had been injured, hurriedly offered a helping hand to the man on the floor, who got to his feet humiliated rather than enraged, raised his hat, excused himself for having disturbed them and lumbered off.

'See – that's the language he understands!' the professor laughed once the gipsy was out of hearing.

'Yes, but I can't go around treating people that way,' Master Törner objected.

'No, I know – and that's why they feel free to be insolent to you. Rabble and dogs need thrashing! If you'd given that rogue a beating your time here would have been more pleasant.'

'But human beings are human beings, all the same.'

'*De omnibus est dubitandum*. You question everything *nisi de plebe* – except the common people – in whom you've somehow placed a sacred trust.'

'Leave the politics out of it,' Törner replied. 'Let me enjoy the pleasure of looking at the face of an honourable man and listening to someone who speaks without lying!'

'There, you see,' retorted the contentious professor, 'you don't take the same pleasure in everyone's company, *ergo* not everyone is the same.'

'That's as it may be, but the world shouldn't be organized in such a way that a small minority enjoys a good life while the majority has such a bad one.

'Each and every man to his allotted place! We can thank God that those who are at the bottom are not at the top! Just look at that ruffian you're dealing with here – he has somehow risen above the place that is rightfully his. Look at the way he mistreats men and beasts. Look at the way he robs the old woman. If he ever gained the power to legislate it would simply be to benefit thieves and rogues. Wait and see: it won't be long before he crawls back down to the level nature and his own character assigned him.'

'Yes, but are those at the top always the best?' queried Törner, a secret opponent of absolutism.

'Not always, but often. And once the best man has come to power he usually gathers the best around him – and then absolutism is good.'

'Absolutism is never a good thing unless it's imposed by a usurper,' Törner explained. 'In which case his ability to overcome obstacles and dangers demonstrates his genius.'

'You're thinking of Cromwell, the Lord Protector, aren't you?'

'Yes. And his ministers and generals. Venner the wine-cooper, Tufnell the carpenter, Okey the batman; and Admiral Deane the odd-job man, Colonel Goffe the baths attendant; that simple soldier Major-General Skippon, and Governor Tickborne the linen-merchant.'

'There you are then, talent achieves the position it merits!'

'True, but only after revolutions. Whereas we had Erik XIV succeeding Gustav I and Kristina succeeding Gustav Adolf.'

'And Karl XI after Karl X; and we saw Cromwell the son disappear like a puff of smoke after Cromwell the father. Constant revolution then – is that what you want?'

'Or an elected dictator!'

'Or settle on a ruler like the Egyptians used to settle on Apis, the Bull of Memphis. Educate him to be a wise man, distance him from all the petty interests of life, coach him as the Japanese coach the Mikado. No, that's not the way. Let life in all its variety produce the man the age needs! After periods of partisan strife and general exhaustion, the absolute ruler the people need will appear with the approval of all. Cromwell as absolute ruler was a greater despot than Charles I, and Fredrik III of Denmark actually led the revolution against the nobility, as Karl XI did here.'

'But our king is an imbecile, an ignoramus who believes in priests and witches!' Master Törner shouted, really letting himself go.

'Quiet, for God's sake!' the professor warned him, looking carefully out through the bushes into the garden, which lay in darkness apart from one or two weak patches of light from the lanterns. 'And as for Cromwell, that abuser of Parliament, didn't he believe in priests? He did, and a good deal more firmly than the constitutional monarch he executed.'

Törner cocked his ear in the direction of the avenue of maple trees: something had moved there and alarmed him. But when everything remained silent he raised his voice again, enjoying this opportunity to get things off his chest. Thumping his beer mug down on the table, he enunciated his favourite dictum – one he had taken from the Cartesian philosophy that had recently made its debut on the European stage:

'*De omnibus est dubitandum*! Down with absolutism, down with Cromwell, down with Karl, that lackey of priests...'

The professor placed his huge hand over Törner's mouth for at that moment Magelone appeared on the bridge leading out to the summerhouse on the lake.

She was dressed in a short-skirted green hunting outfit, fancifully embroidered with spangles and glass beads. Her hair hung wild and disordered about her head which, although not pretty, possessed the softness of youth; but her predatory mouth, plebian nose and lead-grey eyes were frightening and repellent. She was carrying glasses and a serving jug with wine and she bore greetings from Mistress Törner, who had ordered her to serve them this evening as the maids could not be spared from the house and children.

This sounded quite likely although Törner could not hide his surprise at her finery and asked her why she was so dressed up.

The girl thought about her answer for a moment, was embarrassed by the professor's searching look and answered, rather unwillingly, with the truth.

'Jensen said I should.'

So it was her brother who had made her so grand and showy. Well, perhaps it was just vanity.

When she had set the jug down she made to leave but the professor, who was of a humorous disposition, caught her by her tousled hair and forced her to sit down. He offered her a drink from his glass and asked her whether she had any particular accomplishments.

Törner, who did not want her company, answered for her, saying that she was a good cook, as he had discovered during the weeks she had been in his service.

'Yes, but the baroness doesn't give me any food to cook,' the girl interposed, 'and cooking swill for chickens and pigs is no way to get on in the world.'

She said this in a pained childish tone of voice, as if the chance to cook good food was her lifelong dream. Without thinking, and being a man who was easily moved, Törner immediately came up with a solution that would both rescue the girl from the misery in which she lived and free him from her unsettling presence.

'Can't you get her a job as a cook at the Regensen, Bureus? You're the dean, after all.'

'Well, we can certainly think about it,' the professor said, letting go of the girl.

'What's the Regensen?' Magelone asked, full of curiosity.

'It's the refectory where the students eat at the king's table,' Törner replied.

'And you might even get a chance to sleep with young gentlemen!' the professor joked.

This prospect seemed to hold no fears for Magelone – at least, she laughed loudly at the remark.

'Right, off you go now, you cat,' Törner said and pushed her away. 'But if you're going to work in the royal kitchens you're going to have to learn to scrub that dirt off. Right then, away with you!'

Then the two gentlemen settled down to serious drinking and discussing the affairs of the world, though concentrating mainly on their own concerns. Time after time Törner voiced his rage at being compelled to remain in this house of filth and crime but the professor counselled courage and endurance and suggested he make the acquaintance of his neighbours and thus procure information about the district and its inhabitants. There were, after all, only two months left until the beginning of October and then he would be free. He advised him how to deal with the gipsy and, above all, he warned him to take greater care when expressing his opinions, particularly on political matters and the delicate subject of the absolutist government.

At last they rose to retire to bed. On reaching the house they came upon Ivan, who was busy bandaging the leg of the red horse.

'What the devil have you done to the beast?' the professor asked angrily.

Without a moment's hesitation, as if it was a lesson learned by heart, Ivan replied that Jensen had ridden the horse on an errand and the horse had taken fright, shied and thrown its rider. It had then kicked him in the eye severely enough for them to send for the surgeon.

'Everything that happens in this house seems to be a farce,' the professor whispered as they went up the stairs. 'No doubt, what the boy said was all lies, too. But it's none of our business.'

And they went in for a few hours' sleep before the professor rode back to Lund.

*

The dog days came and with them an overpowering heat that caused everything to rot. The whole house stank and swarms of flies hatched in the dung heap, in the gutter, in the pigsty. The garden was so disgusting that Master Törner preferred to remain a prisoner on his balcony. When he took his children for a walk he chose the highway as the only place that was clean, but it was so monotonous, sun-baked, dry and dusty that it offered no refreshment or recreation, and walking in the woods was made unsafe by the presence of marauders.

His efforts to get to know his neighbours failed to lead to the desired results. They received him with only as much courtesy as they were compelled to show and they remained silent. Thus, after a few minutes of doing all the talking himself, he would get up and leave. He could hardly state openly that he was there to sound out their views on Sweden and integration, and they were not inclined to share their thoughts with him. There was something more behind it than mere animosity and indifference towards him as an outsider but he was unable to pinpoint what it was.

Once again he was thrown back on his own company and felt he was a prisoner in the house. On the few occasions he had to go downstairs someone would always accost him, and the need to talk to another human being led him back to the gipsy even though he was now utterly convinced that Jensen was involved in some clandestine business and he feared being drawn into it.

The morning after the arrival of the professor the gipsy had humbly requested Törner to call on him on the ground floor where, in order to protect his eye from daylight, he had shut himself in a darkened room.

He was lying on his bed with bandaged eyes, the table beside him filled with bottles, and he was complaining pitifully about the loss of his eye, kicked out by the horse. He said the surgeon had just visited, cut into the eye and pronounced that he must stay indoors for seven weeks. Törner felt genuine sympathy for the poor wretch and promised to look in on him now and again.

The gipsy thanked him for this and for many other things – indeed, for much more! Törner would, of course, know what he was referring to!

The latter, assuming this to be a reference to his assistance during the previous night's fracas in the summerhouse, carelessly omitted to ask for an explanation.

The following day, however, the gipsy had got up and gone to the summerhouse to meet an elderly man of unpleasant appearance, with whom he ate and drank and finally sang.

So the whole business of the eye was just another piece of theatre, though Törner was unable to divine its purpose since even a child would not be taken in by it.

It was impossible to decide whether the gipsy had laid on this performance as an excuse to ease himself out of the company of the baroness and into a room of his own, or whether it was to gain access to a dark room where he could receive secret visits.

What was quite certain, however, was that he did receive visitors in his new room, the first of them being the elderly man with the sly appearance and the sly manner who, to put it bluntly, gave the impression of having been a convict. The gipsy informed Törner, who was no longer bothering to ask questions, that the man was an official state gardener who had come to inspect the work in the garden, though not to take any part in it. But since cherry-picking was the only work to be done at the moment, it scarcely called for a Royal Gardener with a salary of five hundred marks a month to oversee the younger gardener while he did it. This, then, was another blatant lie, simply to provide the sly visitor with an excuse to remain on the estate in the guise of a gardener.

Then another unexpected and equally inexplicable event occurred: for no apparent reason the gatekeeper was dismissed from his post. On the evening before his departure he put in a rowdy appearance, singing abusive songs about the gipsy and making it clear he was convinced that the gipsy had caused his dismissal and was thus his enemy. Three days later, however, he turned up at Bögely in his best clothes and spent several hours conferring with the baroness and the gipsy. The latter informed Törner that the gatekeeper was trying to embroil him in a plot against the authorities, about which he and the gatekeeper shared some dangerous secrets. After a few days the discussions ceased and the gipsy claimed to have lost interest in getting mixed up in other people's affairs.

All this suggested to Törner that something significant was on the move and in order to untangle the complex web he decided to follow his friend's advice and lull the villains into a sense of false security. With this in mind he set off on his morning walk and went to the spruce tree with the carved inscriptions; once there he cut an arrow through the eye, covered his footprints with pine needles and waited to see what would happen.

Two days later, when the baroness and the factor and the whole household had driven off to a village fair, there was a knock on the door of Torner's tower room.

He shouted 'Come in' and a very old man entered. His face was beardless and pale as plaster, with a host of wrinkles and folds running in all directions. His front teeth were missing and his mouth had shrunk so much that he appeared to be chewing and sucking his lips, which lent him a gruesome skull-like appearance. His clothes were filthy but there were gold trinkets hanging on his watch chain and silver buttons on his coat.

After pretending to be surprised at finding a stranger in the tower room the old man asked for the factor and Master Törner replied that he had just gone out.

'That's strange. He knew I was coming,' the man mumbled.

He then began to bemoan his ill luck and the fact that it would now be impossible for him to inspect the property.

Törner, suspecting yet another piece of duplicity, cheered him up by offering to show him round the place. They went downstairs and Törner made up his mind not to say anything disparaging about the gipsy since the purpose of the skull-faced man's visit seemed to be to elicit Törner's attitude to him. So he took the old man, to all appearances unintentionally, to all the worst places, leading him past the filth without appearing to notice it himself; and whenever the old man shook his head at the ruinous condition of the estate or grumbled at the neglect of the fields he always had an excuse – or, indeed, praise – at the ready.

The old man's visit seemed to have a twofold purpose: to discover where Törner's sympathies lay and to assess the condition and value of the estate. He was beside himself with rage that the property had been rendered valueless, from which Törner concluded he was a money-lender with some kind of preferential rights to the estate.

Finally the stranger asked if there were any carpenters employed there and, if so, what they were working on. Törner assured him that he saw them working away all day but felt unable to answer the second part of the question.

When it was time for him to leave, the stranger asked Törner not to mention his visit and, in return, Törner asked the visitor not to pass on anything he had said.

The gipsy was fooled. The following day he was in a wonderful mood – modest, smiling, full of friendship. He invited Törner to join him in a glass of wine in the summerhouse and Törner found it impossible to refuse.

They began with a relatively drinkable wine, after which Magelone suddenly appeared with a plate of pastries she claimed to have baked herself. She was wearing a low-cut blue dress looped up on one side. After Törner had tasted the offerings and uttered some words of encouragement, the gipsy quickly took advantage of the moment.

'Magelone, thank Master Törner for his help with your future good fortune!'

Magelone quickly tried to kiss his hand, which he withdrew while asking with some surprise why she thought she owed him any thanks.

'Magelone has told me everything, you know. She's like a magpie when it comes to chattering,' the gipsy said.

'And what has she told you?' Törner asked, feeling as if a vice was being tightened on him.

'All that about the royal table, of course!' the gipsy said laughing.

'Oh, Regensen! That was something I just happened to mention but if the girl attaches any value to it I'll be happy to give her a reference.'

'There, you see, Magelone, you have his word on it,' the gipsy jumped in quick as a lawyer and Törner felt himself disagreeably out-manœuvred. In order to formulate his promise more precisely in front of witnesses, Törner added:

'But remember, I'm only giving her a reference and I can't promise her a position because it's the consistory court that makes appointments, not me. And they only do so after strict tests. If she doesn't pass the tests and the court doesn't want her then there's nothing to thank me for and I'll have done nothing but cause her inconvenience.'

Of course, the gipsy agreed, all that was perfectly well understood, but a chance to show her skills was all that Magelone needed since she was without doubt the most accomplished cook in the province, having learned her skills at no less a house than the High Constable's.

At this point Magelone withdrew to the accompaniment of much curtseying, bowing and scraping and the two men were left alone.

The gipsy moved on to a new topic of conversation, one he had never shown an interest in before, *viz* politics. He managed to muddle together Cromwell, Fredrik III and Karl XI and went on to indulge in paeans of praise for the Swedish king.

Törner realized at once that he must have been hiding in the bushes on the evening of the professor's visit. He understood that the gipsy, relying on the fact that the eye on the spruce tree had been blinded, was trying to lure him into making criminal statements, possibly in the presence of witnesses also concealed in the bushes. Törner therefore began an oration on the benefits of absolutism, on Karl XI's immortal services to the kingdom and on a citizen's sacred duties to God, king and fatherland.

Jensen must either have heard very little of that evening's political conversation or have failed to understand any of it, for he suddenly altered course completely and began to berate everything to do with government, with authority, and with the police. Törner set about refuting him on all points, enjoining the gipsy to distinguish in particular between state authority and the administration of the law. He regaled him with complex and learned analyses, conflating disciplines and larding his speech with Latin and Greek quotations so that the gipsy, who was taking it all seriously, became giddy with the effort of trying to comprehend the incomprehensible. But Master Törner was not yet prepared to release him and, digging deep into the hidden corners of his knowledge, he excavated disconnected fragments from Grotius's *Concerning the Law of War and Peace* and Pudendorf's *Concerning the Law of Nature and Nations*, and he gave a detailed account of the whole of Hobbes's famous dissertation *On the Citizen*, in which absolutism is central to the system. He continued in stentorian tones for fully an hour, silencing the gipsy's every effort to interrupt him and finally leaving him sitting there pale and crushed by his superhuman efforts to follow Törner's speech and, above all, to show that he understood it.

When Törner concluded his rhapsody the gipsy nodded appreciatively but was so exhausted he could do no more than hiss: 'Splendid!'

Then he poured down a large glass of wine, cleared his throat and attempted to respond. But the only topics he could cope with were things that were close to home: the baroness, her virtue and justice, and the disgraceful slanders against her; and finally he lost himself in a long-winded, boastful list of all his shabby love affairs, each more unbelievable than the last.

Törner, who was paying careful attention to each and every turn the conversation took, recognized at once that this was the topic the gipsy had been steering towards the whole evening. He kept his ears open so as to be ready when the gipsy at last got to the point.

'Oh yes, there are plenty of girls around if you've got money in your pocket!' the gipsy concluded after a lengthy disquisition.

He donned the knowing look he always wore when he wanted to wheedle secrets out of someone. And then, out it came:

'Suffice it to say, there isn't a girl in the world I couldn't buy for a hundred daler.'

A deathly silence followed these words for the gipsy could not risk going any farther. Törner wondered for a moment whether to unmask the wretch and slap his face for sitting there offering to sell his own sister but, wanting first to be certain of the vileness he suspected, he baited a trap.

'Talking of young girls, Jensen, I think you should keep an eye on Magelone in case Mats leads her astray.'

The gipsy's face grew dark.

'That ruffian, that bumpkin! Just let him try!'

From his window Törner had seen Magelone and Mats playing in the labourer's room: only playing, admittedly, but a not completely innocent game that consisted of throwing one another down on the bed. There was no need for Törner to give the gipsy all the details and he did not want to imply that he knew more than he did.

'All I'm saying is that they play together, but play can turn serious and Mats is just a poor labourer.'

'Oh, damn the girl! If she's going to get herself into trouble – and that seems to be what girls are fated to do – she might at least do it with a gentleman!'

There was no longer any room for doubt: the gipsy wanted to sell his sister to a gentleman and for as little as a hundred daler.

Törner excused himself on grounds of weariness and got up to go to bed. He thanked the gipsy for his hospitality and said goodnight.

*

Back in his room Törner was seized by self-disgust at having shared a table with a thief and pimp. How could he have sunk so low in three months? How could he have been drawn into a circle so inferior to his own and allowed himself to become involved with people and situations of no concern to him? Did it result from the *inertia* that afflicts a mind isolated from its proper environment – when, after a period of resistance, the mind becomes weary and crippled by some sudden undertow that drags inexorably on the will?

As he thought through what he had just experienced, turning it over and over in his mind until he felt helpless, the voice of nature began to speak to the atoms of his fragmented soul. Urges he had repressed for half a year reawakened and, buoyed up by the hope of at last having what he had been deprived of for so long, his instincts grew with terrifying power. The image of the girl in the blue dress emerged as if from a magic lantern, her shoulders bared and her hips and back writhing in fiery, snakelike movements. Memories of the ugliness in her eyes, the spiteful lines around her mouth, the filth that clung to everything about her – these things his mind suppressed. There stirred in him a desire to embrace her roughly, like an animal, like a dog takes a bitch; but at the same time there came a firm resolve never to kiss her.

His imagination depicted everything just as he desired it to happen.

He knew he would never be able to utter words of love to her, would never be able to say anything to her, would not be able to fuse his soul with hers nor look to any future: he would simply act like a sultan and, when he saw she was willing, he would drop his handkerchief, beckon her to come and then step into some dark and concealed corner where no-one could see what happened. Not even he would see, for he would not permit his eyes to be soiled by memories nor his thoughts plagued by clear images. He and she would simply come together as animal with animal and afterwards they would part.

That is how he thought it would happen and that is how he dreamed of it that night.

*

91

When Master Andreas Törner woke the following morning he had
decided to have nothing to do with Magelone. It was not that he
had any strong moral qualms: his sick wife had given him his
freedom in affairs of the flesh and, moreover, they had recently
witnessed the case of a married priest in the diocese who, having
written to the bishop pleading to be released from his marriage
vows, had received permission as requested. But it went against
the grain to enter any kind of relationship with a family of
criminals and he found the idea of having an affair odious when
his family was living in the same house. He was also afraid the
girl might use him to conceal her dalliance with other men.

But the very fact that he was in a position to accommodate his
heathen lusts and was allowing his thoughts to play with that
possibility drew him towards the inevitable. Having to wrestle
against temptation all day meant that temptation grew to
enormous proportions. It wormed its way into his soul and, what
was worse, thoughts of the girl supplanted all other thoughts,
confused his powers of judgment, extinguished his suspicions
about the gipsy's criminal dealings, relaxed the watchfulness with
which he defended himself against the cunning of his enemy, and
lulled him into a sense of security without him even being aware
it was happening.

So, when he heard a terrible din coming from the stables and
hurried to the window, he watched with indifference as the gipsy
threatened the labourer Mats. In self-defence, the latter raised the
shovel he had in his hand and angrily struck the gipsy's arm,
causing him to flee the stable while ordering the labourer to leave
the farm.

With the same unthinking composure he watched Mats pack
his bundle and go. Nothing that happened in the course of the day
was of any real interest to him and everything seemed trivial and
mundane.

He went down to the hothouse and saw the missing dung-cart
standing there with its front wheels stuck fast in the mud and a
load of manure heaped on the ground beside it. If his mind had
been clear he would have made a connection with his earlier

suspicions about the nocturnal activities in the attic and would not have failed to investigate whether the dung heap was being used as a hiding place.

But he only had an eye for one thing and that was the girl. Wherever he went he saw her: he met her on the stairs, met her up in the attic and he could not fail to notice that she had dressed up.

That afternoon Master Andreas Törner had planned to take the children out but the carriage from the inn failed to arrive. The gipsy, however, had just harnessed the horses to his great coach and, since the children were disappointed to be missing their promised trip, the gipsy invited the gentlefolk to join the baroness on her drive in the woods. Törner did not refuse and he felt no surprise at finding himself sitting in the coach an hour later with the whole party and with Magelone opposite him on the back seat. Nor did he find anything offensive in the way the baroness's chatter was all aimed at drawing his attention to the girl, who sat there staring with her grey, button-like eyes, trying to be graceful by making cute faces. But when she grinned the sharp canines that projected in front of her other teeth were bared.

Time after time a gleam of sanity illuminated Törner's mind as he looked at his children in the company of these filthy people who even bore the smell of rotting meat and wet dogs out into the woods with them. An awareness of his awful humiliation dawned on him along the road when he saw passing travellers laughing at his party. Only then did he notice that the baroness was attired in a green silk dress with a catskin collar and wearing a hat from the time of Gustav I, a huge monstrosity that resembled an umbrella topped with a pine-marten's tail. The gipsy was parading his yellow jacket, on the back of which five tarry fingers had left their traces – presumably a souvenir from the row with Mats that morning. The horses looked as if they had come straight out of the Dance of Death in Lund Cathedral and the wheels of the coach were coated in mud and filth even though the weather was good and the sun shining.

For a moment Törner thought of getting out but he calmed down and by fixing his attention on his children he shut out his surroundings, turned a deaf ear to the gipsy's babble, heard nothing but the cheerful laughter of the children and saw only their happy game as they tried to pull a branch from a beech tree whose foliage hung down over the coach. Then he thought of his dear sick wife lying alone at home, ill and confined to her room, while her summer passed without a day free from suffering. He felt shame, sorrow and rage at the pain fate was undeservedly inflicting on him and making him inflict on others, and he was so taken up with these feelings that he failed to notice that the coach had turned off at an inn where a boisterous crowd of people had gathered round a juggler while peasants danced and drank under a beech tree.

He was, however, suddenly wakened by the noisy attention the coach attracted from the crowd, which greeted its arrival with laughter and yelling.

Beside himself with indignation he stood up, grasped the reins and turned the horses so that they went back out on the highway.

There was a moment's silence – a silence so threatening that Törner felt forced to offer the baroness an apology. He excused his behaviour by saying he had promised his wife not to take the children into large gatherings of people, which the baroness – surprisingly amenable – immediately pretended to understand and approve of: indeed, she became fulsome in her praise of his thoughtfulness.

And so they drove home.

Not for a moment did it occur to Törner that the whole business was just another piece of calculated deception. It had all seemed so disgusting and detestable that he repressed all thoughts of it and made himself blind and deaf and impervious to all the unpleasant impressions.

*

After the children had gone to bed at about seven o'clock in the evening, Master Andreas Törner withdrew to his room to be alone and avoid meeting any of the residents of the house. The August evening was warm but dark and he lit a candle, took off his coat and sat down at the table with a book.

Sitting there turning the pages of his *flora* he does not notice how his thoughts are leaping from leaf to leaf seeking somewhere to settle. They flit like bees from flower to flower testing for sweetness with their proboscises until at last his eye is caught by the chapter on the sexual life of flowers. There, for the first time, he begins to take in what he is reading and everything assumes form and life. The secrets of impregnation arouse him as they arouse a schoolboy. All the things he is already familiar with take on a new interest, offer new aspects. And as he reads he senses how the dried-up wells within him begin to fill, how his blood grows hot, how the mighty spirit of nature begins to address him in forceful tones. Lust stirs within him, the urge to experience a pairing in which body and soul emerge from the confined prison of the self and apprehend the life and future of the species, even if only for a few seconds.

Without lifting his eyes from the book he felt someone enter the room. He noticed the slight draught caused by someone moving and breathing in the air of the room and he felt, as it were, a warmth on one side of his body where the sound of creeping footsteps could be heard; and when he turned round he saw Magelone standing in the light, her malicious lead-grey eyes with their bulging cornea, dull and lifeless, reflecting the candlelight.

'What do you want?' Master Törner asked breathlessly. He saw she had dressed up again – in a dress that only a whore would wear.

'Jensen sends his apologies,' she stammered, 'but he's run out of tobacco and wonders if you'll be kind enough to lend him some, Sir?'

'Here!' Törner answered abruptly, stood up and gave her half a pouch.

He thought for a moment as the girl remained standing there. Then he made his decision, but changed it even as he spoke.

'Would you please tell Jensen from me that it is...' (at this point he turned away) '...improper for young girls to visit gentlemen so late in the evening.'

He took the girl by the arm and pushed her towards the door, changing his mind twice before he got her out. And then he regretted he had let her go but it was too late.

One whore is like another, he thought. If it is not this one it will be another one. And if it is not me it will be Mats. Her brother is a thief – but then, no doubt, so are all whores' brothers! What a mess of a family tree!

And with that he had come to his decision for the following evening.

*

Everything happened as he had planned and fantasized but, once the first feeling of strength and lust was past, there came fear and disgust. Fear because he had heard someone moving in the attic and then creeping away, from which he concluded he had been spied on; and disgust – an awful sensation of filth, a sensation so strong that he felt everything had been besmirched, his room, his body, his soul. He would never have believed it possible for anything to be so utterly repugnant and his lust was extinguished by the mere thought of what he had been through.

But now it was done and could not be changed. He had embraced a beast and after the embrace the beast had kissed him like a cat. And he had turned away as if afraid to inhale unclean breath.

*

The following morning he met Magelone on the stairs. She looked at him with indifference and he looked at her as if nothing had happened.

He was glad the affair had left no impression, no disquieting memories, no desire to renew the relationship, no regret, no reproaches.

But in the afternoon Magelone returned and knocked on his

locked door.

He opened the door and asked her to go, for God's sake, go: Jensen might find out about everything and then she would be lost.

'Oh, Jensen already knows about it,' the girl replied and tried to force her way in.

'You can't come in! My wife will send for the police and we'll be in trouble,' he said in embarrassment. The word 'police' had an uncannily rapid effect and the girl disappeared.

That evening Törner and his family were sitting at the table. They had left the doors and windows open to enjoy the last of the evening light and were eating in silence as people tend to when in the company of someone who is ill. Only an occasional softly spoken word passed between them. The sound of song, music and shouting came from a party down in the garden. Visitors for the baroness had arrived early that morning and had immediately started drinking and had continued until noon. Then they slept for a couple of hours, lying here and there among the bushes before resuming their wild antics. From his window Törner had seen the strangers and been amazed at their peculiar appearance: a man the size of a house, with a red nose and bloodshot eyes, and in his company two women who looked like whores or pawnbrokers. According to what was said, he was a carrier and the women were his wife and sister-in-law, old friends of the baroness's parents. It was claimed they were considering buying the estate.

Törner's suspicions about the authenticity of the baroness's birth and status were reawakened. In any event, a baron whose social circle included people like these must have been poverty-stricken, yet the baroness's parents were reputed to have been well-off.

During the course of the day Törner was invited to join the drinking party but made his excuses when he saw that all the guests, women and children included, were drunk. From then on he noticed a certain ill-will, something hostile in the behaviour of the company, although it did not come to open conflict since he took care to keep his distance.

But even as he sat there believing himself safe in the bosom of his family, behind closed doors and well away from the unbridled savages, he suddenly saw Magelone's tousled head poke through the doorway. Her eyes bulged even more than usual and she laughed in the foolish way that drunks have.

'What are you looking for?' he asked quickly, hoping to avert a scandal.

Supporting herself on the furniture the girl moved across the room with a mixture of uncertainty and insolence that frightened Mistress Törner and the children.

'What are you looking for?' Törner repeated, raising his voice.

The girl had reached the table where Mistress Törner was sitting propped up with cushions. Leaning against the chair, her eyes defiant and brazen, she sneered shamelessly at her former mistress as if wishing to savour her revenge on the woman who had once, with good reason, struck her.

Mistress Törner turned away, the colour drained from her face and she fainted. Törner immediately grasped Magelone by the arm, opened the door and shoved her out into the corridor where she flopped down on a pile of bones the dogs had collected from the remains of the day's party. Then he locked the door.

He scarcely had time to revive his wife and help her from the table before someone began pounding on the outer door. The children screamed in terror, upset by these strange and incomprehensible events, and when the knocking continued Törner went to the door and asked who was there.

The gipsy answered in his most cheerful voice, begging Törner's pardon for intruding but saying he had people with him who wanted to view the apartment. It was customary to allow them viewing rights, wasn't it?

Törner saw the malicious, vengeful glint in the gipsy's eyes as he brought in four intoxicated individuals who, with no sign of shame, took advantage of their legal right to cover the tenant's floor with mud and to disturb the domestic peace of a sick woman.

He seethed with rage as these ruffians poked around, pretending to be measuring doors and windows while mumbling the odd word that was supposed to convince him they really had come on their stated errand, whereas in reality they had the greatest difficulty holding back their laughter. This event, trivial as it was, revealed an undercurrent of challenge and arrogant presumption and, so as not to be tempted into an angry outburst, Törner went out on to the balcony and took his children with him.

The gipsy's action was both a declaration of war and a victory parade with all flags flying, for he was demonstrating to his trapped and defeated enemy that he knew he had him fettered hand and foot and, having outwitted him, was placing his filthy heel on his neck. Törner writhed in agony but swore a silent oath that before it finished he would bring the gipsy down, bring him down once and for all. And kill him, not merely wound him, kill him so as not to be killed himself.

He passed the following night pondering ways he could destroy, without any repercussions, this malevolent brute who took callous pleasure in doing evil.

There was no longer any prospect of lulling him into a sense of security. The gipsy did not have those moments of weariness after the work of the day was over when he could be caught unawares; and the relationship between them was now so strained that even a semblance of peace was impossible. To take up arms against an enemy like this meant matching him in ruthlessness, not shrinking from foul means, not being ashamed to snoop into his secrets. It meant listening at doors, coaxing confidential confessions from those close to him – and then using it all. But Master Törner felt incapable of such behaviour. It went against the grain to commit a dishonourable deed and thus injure, perhaps even destroy, his own self-respect. This was a battle he was doomed to lose, but he could neither flee nor cease to struggle for to do so would mean that defeat was immediate.

He felt as the Greeks must have felt when fighting the barbarians – involved in a battle which the barbarians were bound to win because they were less civilized. He felt like Archimedes, who fell at the hand of a common soldier even though, with his computational skills, he could have constructed a machine that blew a thousand soldiers to pieces.

By making an inventory of the gipsy's mental faculties, an inventory of his soul, Törner had uncovered two points at which, in any struggle between them, soul could battle against soul, mind against mind, in a way that offered hope of victory to the mind that was stronger. First and foremost, the gipsy suffered from the fear of the unknown that characterizes half-civilized people and he sought to overcome this fear by believing in the protection of unknown powers. If he could be robbed of this protection, his fear would come to life, his belief in his own good luck would be removed and he would crumble, destroyed. There could be no doubting the strength of his belief that he was favoured by fate since, notwithstanding the economic ruin that faced him at Michaelmas, he did not cultivate the soil: he did nothing but lie there with his mouth open waiting for manna from heaven. Törner had no idea whether he believed in the Christian god or not and he had never seen him go to church; on the other hand, he put out milk for his grass-snakes and treated them with religious veneration.

So the snakes must be exterminated and with them the gipsy's belief in their protective powers. Then his fear of an adverse fate would cripple him.

The second point was more difficult but, if Törner could accomplish it, the gipsy's death was certain. By commingling his blood with that of a noble family this pariah had, as it were, boosted his own life-force. His perception that he was related to the nobility had given him a high opinion of himself and, as long as he believed that the baroness really was what she claimed to be, he could hold his head high. But Master Törner was firmly convinced that there was a secret the gipsy was unaware of: he was certain the baroness had lied to her lover and that she was not the scion of a noble line. Time and ingenuity were all that were needed to research this and a study of the parish registers would enable Törner to establish the truth. If his suspicions could be verified, the gipsy would feel deceived and be provoked into committing indiscretions, and who knows what might come to light when two such people began to uncover one another's secrets. Moreover, when the gipsy saw he had been duped by the only person he trusted, when the hopes on which he had built his strength and vitality had been destroyed, his vital flame would fade and die.

*

The act of adding quicksilver to the grass-snakes' milk amounted to no more than the eradication of vermin but Master Törner nevertheless felt uneasy about it. Rather as if he had committed murder or theft, although no-one would ever talk of murdering rats, for instance.

Later, standing at his window to watch the results, he was worried. He had been working for three hours before he heard the sounds of a disturbance issuing from the hothouse. Ivan was the first to discover the disaster and sound the alarm, and the gipsy, who was sleeping off his drunkenness in the bushes, came rushing to the scene. The storm broke first on the head of the gardener, who cursed and swore he was innocent. The baroness, who came running up, was beside herself and wept. Unable to find any signs of violence on the snakes – which had almost crawled out of their skins – and not suspecting anyone might have poisoned animals that could easily have been killed with a stick, these superstitious people at first assumed that some kind of snake plague had broken out. No sooner was plague mooted than they assumed the intervention of fate or of unknown powers.

They gathered up the corpses carefully, placed them in a piece of woollen cloth and carried them into the house.

Through the open windows Törner could hear them lighting a fire in the stove in the hope that heat might resuscitate the corpses.

It was as if the house had been struck by a thunderbolt. People went round in terror, all work came to a halt, the carpenters looked out through the basement windows, and the dogs, which were all for making a meal of the snakes, were ejected to the accompaniment of much noise and fuss and locked up in sheds

101

and outhouses.

There was so much wailing, argument and discussion downstairs that the midday meal remained uncooked and everything was in disarray.

'Ill luck is upon us!' With these words the gipsy concluded his melancholy reflections and proceeded to break open a firkin of spirits, sit down, drink and sing laments until, one by one, the whole family joined him sitting and drinking at the window.

Quite how effective his attack had been became clear to Master Törner that evening when he met the gipsy, now gentle, courteous and humble: it was as if all his hatred had been blown away along with his belief in his good fortune. Ashamed to show weakness and knowing that Törner would laugh at his superstitions, the gipsy made no reference to the grass-snakes.

Instead, in vague and uncertain phrases, he poured out an account of his undeserved misfortunes and spoke of his imminent ruin.

Then he suddenly changed tack and began recounting his love affairs, cobbling together off the top of his head a humorous tale of a gentleman unable to satisfy his mistress, for which reason she became unfaithful.

Törner pretended not to see the point but joined in in the same vein and served up the story of a man who thought he was getting a virgin but caught crabs instead.

The gipsy dodged the attack and began to talk about the carrier who had visited recently and who wanted to buy the estate for sixty thousand daler.

'Of course,' he added scornfully, 'this estate is plenty good enough for a horse-trader.'

Törner let the lie pass without comment but the term 'horse-trader' stuck in his memory and would come in handy later.

*

By the following week Master Törner had completed his clandestine examination of the parish registers and discovered that Baroness Ivanoff had been born into a distinctly non-aristocratic family called Ivarsson. Her father had been no more than a common money-lender, as well as owning two brothels in Copenhagen, where her mother had been a whore.

It came as no surprise when the priest and the registrar confirmed these facts. It could scarcely be otherwise, he thought, in spite of his belief that everything, except the sanctity of the 'common man', was open to question. This love of filth, of lies, of superstition could not have existed in a family in which generation after generation had been raised in a cultured environment. An honoured name usually acts as a spur to great deeds, to some refinement of thought and feeling, or at least to a certain care of one's own person. And before a noble family fell into spiritual decay, it was usually undermined by economic decline, which was not the case here.

During the week Törner spent on his investigations he had ample opportunity to observe how the gipsy had lost his self-confidence and his restless desire for activity. Most of his time was spent lying on the roof of the privy, sunning himself among the rabbits and smoking and sleeping. It was difficult to understand why he had chosen that particular location: perhaps his southern blood was attracted to the heat that rose from the copper sheets of the roof, or perhaps his pariah nature was drawn to the smell there with its reminiscences of putrefaction, excrement and garbage. And the more the gipsy's apathy increased, the more the estate drifted aimlessly. The chickens died by the dozen from starvation and neglect and lay half-rotting on the ground. The dogs hunted the hens and ducklings and took them for food. The sheep fell ill from lying in their own filth, which lay piled a foot deep on the floor; and no-one either watered them or took them out to grass.

The head-gardener, the labourer and the carpenters sat in the cherry trees munching cherries. They picked a full basket for the market but let it stand until the whole lot rotted.

All the while weeds grew in the garden and spread their seeds. Dirt covered the yard, the flies multiplied and the whole house showed the signs of dissolution and decay. Time after time the gipsy roused himself just sufficiently to instigate some new piece of mischief to annoy his tenants: he drove wet dogs up and down the stairs after they had been scrubbed, scattered bones and rubbish in the corridors, let the hens come indoors, caused unnecessary noise at night, and set the dogs on Törner's milkman and postman.

All this simply stiffened Törner's resolve as he made cold-blooded preparations to discharge his second volley – this time with the aim of sinking his enemy for once and for all.

To carry out his plan he chose Magelone, whose hostile attitude he had succeeded in softening with kind words, a task made easier by the maltreatment she suffered from her brother and the baroness, for whom she nursed a deep hatred.

When Magelone was told the results of Törner's investigations she was overjoyed. This was a wonderful opportunity for her to take revenge on the baroness, who would be humiliated, and on her brother, who would lose the spurious lustre that had allowed him to lord it over his siblings.

The row began one Friday evening and Master Törner sat in his window and listened to how it first kindled and then burst into flame. The baroness, alias Miss Ivarsson, was standing at her window flicking dead siskin out of the cages when Jensen enters the room.

There is silence for a moment and then she says:

'Well, Peder, are you going into town tomorrow to buy food?'

'No,' replies the gipsy, 'you can do it yourself!'

'What am I going to buy it with now you've had all my money?'

'Have I? What have I had? What have I actually had for slaving my fingers to the bone for you year in year out without any pay? What have my brother and sister had for being unpaid labourer and maid here?'

Then the woman started. She talked for half an hour, sometimes yelling, sometimes weeping, sometimes swearing.

The gipsy attempted to interpose a word here and there, but in vain. Then he leapt up and rushed out slamming the door behind him. He came back in and hurled out a string of words, among which it was only possible to catch the occasional 'slut as a mother', 'whore' and 'money-lender'.

This set the woman raging for another half an hour and Törner could hear nothing but the distant, cannon-like bang! bang! bang! of the door as the gipsy ran in and out like a madman.

Magelone was then called to the scene. First the baroness cuffed her round the head and then the gipsy did the same. But she refused to surrender: instead, she fired a salvo that echoed through the whole house and could be heard out in the garden, where the men were standing listening behind the bushes.

Now all the old stories came out, going back to the days when the gipsy's parents had lived on the estate and wreaked havoc: accusations of horse-theft, chests whose locks the baroness was supposed to have picked, financial transactions, embezzlement. In short, crooked dealings of every imaginable kind.

The gipsy's voice could no longer be heard and it sounded as if he had left the scene.

The outburst ended with Magelone being thrown out of the house, being publicly called a slut and accused of having had relations with all the men on the estate (with the exception of Törner). She packed her bags and departed.

The fox's lair had been blown wide open and Törner's knock-out blow had created the desired effect.

Pleased and satisfied with his work he went to bed and slept peacefully for the first time in a long time, for he believed that the enemy forces were so shattered and riven by internal strife that they would now leave him in peace.

*

Without knowing it he had timed his grand attack at a particularly opportune moment to cause havoc in the enemy camp. The following day was a Saturday, when the staff would normally have received their wages and the household provisions for the following week been bought. Törner's blow had thus fallen at a point when the gipsy's mind was already overwrought and incapable of dealing with the many and various pressures afflicting it: he was in complete disarray and this would have been the end of him if outside forces had not come to his aid.

Törner went down to the yard the morning after this disturbance and he met the head-gardener, who was upset and ready to open his heart. Since Törner wanted to hear the results of his thunderbolt, and since he assumed that all danger was now past, he asked the gardener whether he had heard the previous evening's row.

Yes, he had, and he wanted to warn Master Törner about the baroness and the gipsy. Now that he recognized the kind of people he was living among, he felt no hesitation in telling him that the gipsy and the baroness had broken into his room in his absence and opened his writing case with forged keys.

Törner was beside himself with rage and wanted to go to the constable without delay, but the gardener restrained him and asked whether he had heard about the theft of a horse from one of their neighbours during the night.

He had not, and so the gardener told him the details.

It had been dark when the time came for Magelone to go over to the inn to arrange transport back to her parents' home and the gardener and the labourer had promised to keep her company. They were walking together down the highway and had reached the farm from which the horse had just been stolen when they heard cautious footsteps behind them and noticed the gipsy creeping along the roadside ditch in disguise, his hat pulled down over his face and a black object in his hand, which from a distance looked as if it might be a shoe. They turned their backs on him and pretended not to notice him. But they heard him following them all the way to the inn, where he disappeared from sight.

The head-gardener had lain awake that night and heard the gipsy come out into the yard around one o'clock and order up two horses – one for himself and one for the labourer, whom he ordered to accompany him. It was three o'clock, however, before the gipsy appeared and then he and the labourer had ridden to the gipsy's parents' home at Vidala taking various small items that Magelone had left behind. On their return he ordered the labourer to keep their trip secret – but probably meant him to talk about it, which he duly did.

Master Törner said nothing when he heard this story, made no comment at all and pretended to go up to his room. He turned back halfway, however, and set off for the farm from which the horse had been stolen. On his way there he reminded himself of all the things the gipsy had said over the months and everything that had happened: all of it served to reinforce his conviction that Jensen was the thief.

He remembered that, at the beginning of the summer, Jensen had gleefully told him stories about horse-theft and had described the theft of a red horse from the same farmer in particular detail. He remembered the tricks that, according to the gipsy, were used to make stolen horses completely unrecognizable – slashing the forehead, for instance, so that a blaze grew in. He remembered that they had found the dun horse with a cut on its forehead a month ago and been unable to understand who had done it or what the point was. And lastly, and significantly, there had been the horse-dealer's visit that dreadful Sunday.

All this fitted together neatly and pointed in one and the same direction – all except the cut on the dun's forehead, which did not seem to fit into the picture.

Why had it been slashed? Was it a stolen horse being rendered unrecognizable in order to be sold? This horse had a peculiar habit of going everywhere at a gallop, as Törner had noticed when he travelled to Landskrona with the gipsy. The gipsy had offered a strange explanation for the horse's bad habit: it had, he claimed, been broken in by a milk-carrier. It seemed more likely to Törner, however, that the horse's speed might have to do with its driver's fear that it could be the object of close examination if it moved at a slower pace.

He put that incident aside, however, as simply complicating matters. The most important thing was to find proof in the present case and, with that in mind, he set off for the field from which the horse had disappeared.

He soon located the spot where the horse had been led out of the field before being taken away in the opposite direction to Bögely. He attached little weight to this – as tricks go, it was pretty basic.

In the clover field he found the hole left by a stake to which the animal had been tethered and he was able to pick out the hoof-prints of the stolen horse. He also discovered impressions left by the thief's feet in the damp ground. A large, clumsy foot, very wide across the sole. Among these tracks there were other deeper ones: regular impressions, much too regular to have been made by the feet of a man leading a horse. More to the point, all the tracks had been made with the same right shoe. It was quite clearly a false trail laid by the thief with a shoe he had brought with him for that purpose and it was very unlikely that the matching half of the pair would turn up at the thief's house! And there, on top of a slightly trampled tuft of clover, lay the shoe, left behind as a misleading *corpus delicti*.

The thinking behind this was not utterly stupid and might possibly have fooled anyone but Törner who, of course, had only just been informed that the gipsy was seen creeping along the ditch the evening before carrying a dark object resembling a shoe. So that others would not be misled by it, Törner took the shoe and threw it as far as he could, after which he lay on the ground and took a cast of the real footprint with the sulphur he had brought with him. With the sulphur cast in his pocket he went home.

On arriving home he pretended to have lost his knife and walked round all the garden paths searching until he found the footprint he needed. He took a cast of it and the two casts matched in every respect, down to the telling detail that the left side of the shoe revealed loose threads of cobbler's wax which had been pressed into the leather sole in the shape of an eyelet.

So it was the gipsy's foot that had left its imprint in the field – *ergo*. *Ergo* what? Was it conclusive proof he had stolen the horse? No, for the gipsy might have gone there to investigate the scene of the crime even earlier than Törner: the fact that Törner's footprints were now in the clover field did not, after all, demonstrate that *he* had stolen the horse.

How, then, was he going to ensnare the gipsy? The only proof the police would accept would be for the horse to be found in the thief's possession. Even that could easily be explained away if the thief claimed to have caught a stray horse. And it was certain that the horse was not going to be found in the gipsy's stable; it might, however, be in the Hälsingborg carrier's stable. Or, there again, possibly not.

Master Törner decided to wait for two days, sleep on it for two nights, and then act!

*

The next day he did not see the gipsy, who was said to be away. He reappeared up on the roof of the privy on the morning of the second day, making a lot of noise and cracking his whip as if enjoying his power over the animals down in the yard. He was half-drunk and very excited. He hurled obscure, defiant words first at the baroness's window and then at Törner's: references to a fox that goes hunting for hens but is tricked; to learned gentlemen who imagine they know everything when they actually don't know any more than he could fit on his thumbnail; to whores and money-lenders who call themselves counts and barons but don't have as much as a clean rag to wear; to simple, ordinary folk who could rise to greatness if they so desired.

At this point he took a swig from his bottle and began singing at the top of his voice 'I am the Count of Luxembourg', which song Törner had not heard for several months. At the end of each verse he cracked his whip and danced on the copper roof so that it boomed and swayed under his weight.

Törner tried to fathom out what lay behind this reckless behaviour. The gipsy's song rang with the triumphant pride of a victor and his insolent challenges suggested he was certain he had gained the upper hand.

Later in the day the gipsy was to be seen sitting alone in the summerhouse playing the hurdy-gurdy with all eight dogs gathered around him. In the evening he caused a ferocious row down in Miss Ivarsson's room, screamed for a quarter of an hour without a pause, slammed the door and broke glass and china. When night fell he put on a horrendous show up in the attic, firing off his gun, dancing on stilts and smashing furniture – all in an effort to provoke Törner into conflict.

Finally he tired of it and went out to the meadow, where he set fire to turf and weeds that were lying there waiting to be burnt, lay down on the dewy ground and seemed to fall asleep.

Törner, on the other hand, could not get a wink of sleep and the longer he lay there plagued by sleeplessness the more determined he became to take direct action against the schemes of his enemy. When morning came, he dressed and set off to pay a visit to the constable: if nothing else, he would report the inhabitants of the house for using forged keys.

*

He was making his way through the beech-wood and had reached the path through the spruce-trees when the cry of magpies drew his attention to the tree that had been used as a message board. He crept into the thicket and soon found it. Where the bark had been skinned off a new symbol had been carved and he was now sufficiently well-versed to interpret its meaning. All the earlier signs had been erased and in their place someone had drawn a fox with its neck caught tight in a snare and its tongue hanging out of its mouth.

Judging by the gipsy's victory dances and noisy arrogance there could be no doubt that the fox was intended to represent Törner.

Driven by a desire to find out exactly where he stood, he hurried on to the constable's house, which he nevertheless approached with some uncertainty since all the magistrates in the conquered provinces were Danes – a concession on the part of the government so that the subjugated population would not live in constant fear of arbitrary and unjust administration of the law. It was, in any case, essential for them to be thoroughly familiar with the local language in order to be capable of following and assessing the nuances of every word.

He passed through the wood and was approaching the village where the constable lived when the gipsy came galloping down the village street on a sweating nag, greeted him with a victorious smile and, leaving him no time to jump aside, splashed mud from the road all over him.

Törner's spirits were at a low ebb and he was plagued by troubled premonitions as he stood there with his hand on the door-knocker. His spirits fell further when the constable met him with a surprised and suspicious expression and led him into a low room in which most of the floor was taken up by dark furniture and two large tables. It was stiflingly hot and, as if to let out some of the heat, the constable opened the door to the adjoining room, went in there for a moment and then returned.

He invited Master Törner to sit down and looked him over from head to foot as if to compare him with the description he had been given and with his own preconceptions. He said nothing, however, and waited calmly for Törner to speak first.

Finally Törner began to speak, rather reluctantly as he was afraid of becoming entangled in contradictions or saying too much. He had really only come prepared to answer questions, in which case the answers would have come of their own accord.

'The reason for my visit,' he began, 'is my landlord, Jensen, the factor at Bögely, whose behaviour has been unacceptable.'

Here he fell silent and waited for a response but none came, only a nod that invited him to continue.

'It's come to my knowledge,' he was forced to go on, 'that the people I'm living with broke into my room and opened my writing-case with forged keys.' At this point he fell silent again.

The constable's expression remained unchanged, indifferent, as if hearing things he was already familiar with.

'And now,' Törner said finally, 'I want them charged with

breaking and entering.'

The constable waited for a moment and then asked:

'What was it that was stolen?'

'Nothing was stolen,' Törner replied. He could not risk claiming that secrets might have been stolen since that could be taken to mean he was in possession of dangerous secrets.

'Are there any witnesses?' the constable asked.

'The head gardener states he heard Jensen's brother and sister talking about it.'

'Just talk, then. And siblings can't stand as witnesses. Nothing stolen, no witnesses, no broken locks! So nothing to base a case on!'

Törner sat there thinking about his accusation, the basis of which had been blown away without trace. He quickly pulled himself together, recognizing that he was showing himself in a bad light – as the kind of man who throws round accusations on very weak evidence. So as not to appear a pathetic wretch he decided to give a fuller account of his dealings with the gipsy.

'Do you really believe, Constable, that Jensen is an honest man who is above all suspicion?'

'There can be no doubt Jensen's been suspected of a variety of things but he's always managed to account for himself,' the constable answered emphatically. 'He was named as the suspect in a case of horse-theft the other evening but the *corpus delicti*, a shoe left behind by the thief, proved not to fit his foot. He also produced an *alibi*: he could prove he was out riding with the farm-labourer at the time the crime was committed; and it's been established that he visited his parents the same night. The fact that he was seen creeping along the ditch in disguise that evening has another explanation altogether.'

'And what's that, if I may ask?'

The constable fixed Törner with a stern and enquiring look and answered in a disapproving tone:

'He was trying to get at the truth as to whether someone very dear to his heart has been seduced with false promises! That's what he was doing!'

A dreadful silence followed. The room danced in front of Törner's eyes and the panes in the windows took on the form of a net in which he was trapped. One thing was clear to him: he had woven the net himself, just as he had nourished at his breast the serpent that was now biting him. He felt powerless. He could not, of course, admit that he was the one who had enlightened the thief about *alibi* and *corpus delicti* and the trick of admitting to something trivial to clear oneself of the main charge. And the business with the girl, while certainly not punishable in law, was quite sufficient to throw suspicion on him and invalidate him as a witness, with the result that any effort he made to give a full explanation of the circumstances would only worsen his situation and involve him in even more contradictions.

The constable, who saw that Törner had been unhorsed, took the opportunity to kick him *in optima forma*.

'As for Jensen,' he added, 'I know he's a half-crazy individual but he has a kind heart and a forgiving nature. Didn't he intercede on behalf of the gatekeeper, his bitterest enemy, who'd robbed him and was threatened with gaol? No, he's not dangerous. As long as the desire for revenge doesn't get the upper hand in a man's mind and make him irrational, then everything will be just fine!'

Törner's ears burned. Many years had passed since he had last been treated as a schoolboy. Boiling with indignation he forgot all the proprieties and began to interrogate the constable.

'What about the peacock, then, and the turkey and the duck and the dung-cart and the things that were removed from the attic at night? And the trip to buy chickens in Denmark? Perhaps you know all about those things, too, Constable?'

'I really don't need to submit to this kind of interrogation but I'll tell you anyway. As far as the peacock, turkey and duck are concerned, a certain individual is under suspicion though proof is lacking – as yet! (Here the constable gave Törner a look that made him go pale.) The thief is clearly a man of some learning since he knew about leaving a false *corpus delicti*, knew that an *alibi* is the most important piece of evidence, and knew – and was also prepared to teach other people – that servants cannot be called as witnesses.'

Törner was now bristling with rage and the angrier he became the more everything spun round in his mind. Aware of his situation, he became so confused that he sat there like a criminal with a bad conscience faced with detection.

The constable continued, quite certain he was on the right track.

'As for the journey to Denmark, on the basis of entries in his notebook Jensen has proved that he undertook that journey for the reasons stated. I've read it with my own eyes and it says: "Friday, 2nd August. Travel to Denmark. Have ten daler with me. Pick up five daler in Landskrona. Buy seventy-five hens."'

At this point Törner raised his head to speak but the skein was already so tangled that he lost all desire to try to untangle it and found himself unable to voice any of the objections he wished to make. He could not say: 'Constable, the very fact that the man is foolish enough to write "travel" and "have" in the present tense whereas normal people usually write after the event – "yesterday", "on such and such a day I was there" – that fact alone seems suspicious.' Nor did he dare explain to the constable the dubious nature of the statement that the gipsy was taking so-and-so much money with him and then picking up so-and-so much more; and he could not bring himself to point out that it was supposed to have been a hundred hens whereas the notebook only referred to seventy-five. He was speechless in the face of such brazenness and listened as in a dream to the constable's proof of the lawful purpose for which the dung-cart was used: the gipsy had been given permission by the Landskrona slaughterhouse to transport pig offal. Törner, however, could still recall the gipsy's claim about the royal stable in Hälsingborg, and in his mind's eye he saw the estate dung-heap – and that certainly could not have come from a slaughterhouse!

The hearing came to an end. Törner rose to leave, now a suspected thief, a false accuser, a man under surveillance, but the constable had one final cut to deliver.

'So I can do nothing for you as far as your writing-case is concerned. But bear this in mind in the future: if you are concealing dangerous state secrets, make sure you keep them well-hidden. I may be Danish-born but I am now a Swedish citizen and, as a loyal subject of my present Lord and King, I will not spare anyone or shrink from any measures necessary to protect and defend the sanctity of the realm to which I have sworn an oath of loyalty.'

Törner left feeling as if he had been horse-whipped. His hands were tied, his honour lost, all hope of recovery gone; sullied, with no prospect of absolving himself; the more he scrubbed at the stain, the more ingrained it became. Even if he found all the proof he needed he could not risk taking action for fear of bringing misfortune on his family; and, moreover, it looked as if the gipsy was intending to issue a legal summons against him. He might be accused of being an accessory to theft since he had taught the thief how to steal; he could be accused of rape or of having seduced an innocent virgin – anything was possible because it would be easy enough for them to produce false witnesses. Worst of all for him, and the surest way for them, was to accuse him of lese-majesty, since he *had* committed that crime and his sense of honour would prevent him denying it.

He had been beaten by a wretch, a wastrel, a vagrant, whose sole advantage lay in being ruthless in his choice of methods. A rational man, learned and honourable, had fallen victim to an ignorant man, who had been quite unaware of the philosophy of crime or the technique of robbery or the procedures of law. Törner, a man who had been robbed, wronged, tormented and persecuted, had been branded; and a thief, a seducer, spy and usurer, who lived on the proceeds of his body like a whore and who was willing to sell his sister as a whore, had become the good man with a noble, forgiving heart, a tender heart, a brother grieving for his sister's lost innocence.

Törner walked along the highway, head bowed, gripping his stick so tight that his fingernails went white. There was only one thing on his mind. He had been accused of seeking revenge.

Revenge for what? A thief had burgled him, had broken his contract, had mocked and persecuted him, and all he had done was report the thief. Surely that constitutes self-defence? Is it not a citizen's duty to report thieves? But now, if the law would do nothing for him, he would avenge himself. Laws are intended to prevent people taking the law into their own hands but against this primitive creature he would have to do it himself, as in primitive times. The destruction of vermin, the eradication of a monster in human guise, the prevention of criminal misdeeds – these were things he could justify to his own conscience. He would set to work with all the superiority of his knowledge and slay this barbarian, not with powder and shot but by means that would leave no trace and bring no punishment down on his own head. He felt he had been on the right track when he unpicked the gipsy's soul and, if circumstances had not come to the gipsy's aid, he would have destroyed him. But devoid of energy and hope as the gipsy was now, and with destitution knocking at his door, his downfall was imminent. His crude soul, seemingly so robust, was no more than a loose structure of poor timbers and, given the blows it had already suffered, a few more shocks would cause it to collapse. What those shocks would be, Master Andreas Törner determined to devise during a night of solitary thought.

*

He had reached the gate without raising his head when the gipsy, who was standing leaning on the fence in an arrogant pose, called to him. When Törner responded to his greeting in cool tones, the gipsy nodded casually without raising his hat and walked towards him wearing his most spiteful grin. He took Törner by the arm with an intrusive familiarity he did not usually show and accompanied him along the avenue. He began talking of financial matters, then came straight to the point and asked whether Törner could advance him a loan of fifteen hundred silver daler.

Törner, who did not in fact possess a penny more than his salary, thought no purpose would be served by wasting time on

116

futile excuses and assured him it would be a pleasure to help him out with such a trivial sum within three days. Then he attempted to escape and go to his room. But the gipsy did not release his grip on his arm; instead he forced him down onto a bench at the table on the grass in front of the house – a position which gave the best view of the high road.

'Sit down and have a glass of wine with us,' the gipsy invited him in a voice that brooked no contradiction.

'Thank you, dear Jensen,' Törner replied, 'but I don't drink before noon.'

'There is no point in saying no, Master Törner, for you *are* going to have a glass. Otherwise I might assume you think you're too good for us. And you're not, are you?' the gipsy said in a carefully modulated humorous tone.

At that moment Miss Ivarsson and Ivan arrived with a jug and glasses and joined them at the table without asking leave and with no sign of the respect Törner had previously enjoyed.

Their intention seemed to be to subject him to some new torment, perhaps by showing him off to travellers along the highway or perhaps simply by taunting him into committing an indiscretion.

The gipsy poured a glass of the rotten-apple wine, drank some and smacked his lips.

'That's my authentic Burgundy I'll have you know!'

'Yes, it's a good wine,' Törner answered mechanically, suppressing his rage by thinking of his plan.

Ivan and the woman made no effort to conceal their laughter.

Then the gipsy poured spirits into the glasses.

'That's not going to pass my lips!' Törner said decisively.

'Isn't it? Oh, come on. If I ask you? Ask you nicely, not force you or threaten you? Lordy, it wouldn't occur to me to threaten you! Never do that, especially in front of witnesses – even if they are invalid as witnesses. No, I'm not threatening you, not even a little bit! Come on now, just a drop!'

Törner laid down his stick to avoid the temptation to commit murder, but he did not drink.

The gipsy emptied his glass and it went straight to his head.

'Now I'm going to sing you a little song!' he shrieked and cleared his throat.

And off he went with his old refrain, 'I am the Count of Luxembourg'.

It was as if this insignificant, cowardly, weak individual had absorbed all the courage and strength his stronger and more substantial opponent had lost. When the gipsy sensed he had Törner under his boot, he felt himself to have grown at least a foot in stature. At the same time, however, he had a vague perception of the insecurity of his position, a premonition that his defeated opponent might rise up and strike down his tormentor. So as to retain a belief in his own superiority the gipsy had to feel his foot constantly on the neck of his defeated enemy, but the more he stamped the firmer Törner's resolve became. The pressure of the heel forced him to think new thoughts – deep, courageous and just – and, growing in strength, they all focused on the same point. Every word the gipsy uttered, every move he made, became a strand in the rope with which he would be hanged. With every minute that passed Törner's assurance and calmness grew.

The drunken bawling brought Törner's children out onto the balcony and they looked down in amazement at their father sitting drinking with the people of the house in the middle of the morning.

'Oh, look, God's little angels!' the gipsy said with genuine admiration.

It was characteristic of this savage to have no concept of the personal value of children or women: he conceived of them as higher, almost celestial beings, like grass-snakes. To the gipsy, children – those small savages, miniature criminals, whose amiability consists in hiding their faults and whose apparent virtue depends solely on the privilege of not having to struggle for the means of survival – offered an image of the highest beings, of the angels, possibly because they could do him no harm and possibly because they showed him the same trust and openness as they showed to everyone else.

'Oh, do let the children come down,' he suggested, wanting to show his tenderness, or perhaps simply to demonstrate how close he felt to these children of a more favoured race, a race he regarded with superstitious respect and to which he had always tugged the forelock.

'They may not come down!' Törner answered.

'Who said they may not?' demanded the gipsy in a threatening voice.

'I did!' Master Törner said sharply. But a moment later he regretted the defiant tone of his refusal and quickly turned it into a joke, something that never failed to remind the gipsy that Törner could read his mind and thoughts.

'Isn't it enough that their father is behaving like a swine? Is it necessary for the children to do the same?' Törner said.

This time, however, his shot missed its mark for it made the gipsy feel that he too was being classed as an animal, which was too forceful a reminder of his true worth.

'Come on down, little ones!' he shouted up to the balcony, turning his back on Törner.

Miss Ivarsson, who had been sitting there in silence, clearly humiliated and oppressed by the events of the past days, now opened her mouth and, with a cry of pain and genuine concern, grasped the gipsy's sleeve and said:

'No, Jensen, let the children be! Children are sacred, like animals!'

In spite of her less than accurate comparison Törner immediately recognised the genuineness of this outburst of maternal feeling on the part of the old woman and he gave her a grateful look, which she rejected since she blamed him for her fall from grace and for the abuse that had resulted from it. But her unexpected intrusion offered the gipsy a target for his cruelty and he turned on her with a snort of rage. He was about to strike her when an unexpected sight came into view on the highway and caught his attention.

A funeral cortège was passing. Six men were carrying a coffin, followed by a woman in black and a small boy. The coffin was

119

painted white and decorated with a green spruce wreath. The woman in mourning wore a long white veil, otherwise everything was black.

'It's the gatekeeper,' Miss Ivarsson said.

At the sight of his enemy's bier (they had become enemies again immediately after their reconciliation) a cry of victory forced its way from the deepest recesses of the gipsy's heart as if he was witnessing the burial of a dangerous witness. His inborn fear of death was momentarily overcome by an irrepressible outburst of joy and he turned and faced the highway, burst into raucous laughter and clapped his hands. Master Törner recognized that this merely veiled the gipsy's secret terror and it gave him an idea – to which he gave physical expression when he saw the grieving woman stop and raise her hands to the heavens as if she was calling down protection or revenge. Miss Ivarsson hid her face in her hands from shame and concern at the gipsy's coarse behaviour.

But Master Törner rose from the bench, removed his hat and stood in a respectful pose until the cortège had passed.

The gipsy was upset by this reproof and asked in a bitter voice:

'What's that farce supposed to mean?'

'That was no farce,' Törner replied unctuously. 'I always pray for the dead.' And he added with emphasis: 'For no-one knows what comes after death, and those who have escaped their punishment in this life can expect to receive it in the next.'

The gipsy, who lived in real terror of a life beyond this one, was reluctant to give in to his fear and, in a last attempt to dull his anxiety, he screamed after the cortège:

'To Hell with you, gatekeeper! To Hell with you!'

'Beware, Jensen, beware!' Törner said. 'The dead may come back and haunt you if you disturb their rest!'

And calm as a future victor who has attacked his enemy's weakest point, happy as a philosopher who has achieved clarity after a long struggle, Törner rose, adopted his sternest professorial manner and repeated in prophetic tones the prediction which he himself intended to bring to fulfilment:

'The dead may come back and haunt you!'

As he walked briskly in through the door he heard – after a moment's silence which showed that his words had had their effect – a loud laugh followed by a reminder about the loan, which was now stated to be a thousand daler. Master Törner turned on the step and nodded his agreement.

*

After much thought Master Andreas Törner had come to recognize that the methods he had been using to destroy this primitive creature had been too refined: he had miscalculated by grossly overestimating the gipsy's sensitivity to moral shame. He had been playing on a sense of honour that either was not present or was so ductile that even the hardest of blows could not shatter it. He saw now that he needed to resort to harsher and simpler methods, the old and tested methods that the church – particularly the popish church – had always employed to make the human soul compliant: man's fear of the life to come. The gipsy with all his superstitions offered fertile soil for such an approach and, thanks to the incident of the funeral cortège and the events that followed, the whole plan and its execution became self-evident.

Hidden away among his possessions Törner had an apparatus recently invented by the Jesuit Athanasius Kircher for obscure but no doubt thoroughly Jesuitical purposes: the *laterna magica* or magic lantern. With its assistance it was possible to produce images in light on walls or smoke or any other background of sufficient density. Törner had often thought of using the apparatus to entertain the gipsy and his companions but had refrained from doing so as he was not inclined to show any kind of generosity to a man who was a thief and who never expressed gratitude. But now, to ensure his own survival, he could use it to achieve a goal that, after four months of suffering, he felt justified in using any available means to attain. He was quite certain that his survival was of greater value to his family and to society than the survival of the verminous creature on whom no-one's well-being

121

depended and whose annihilation could well be the salvation of many.

As he sat there painting shapes on the glass plates Törner had an unpleasant sense that what he was doing was dishonourable. He felt rather like an executioner, a hangman, a torturer or a scavenger. To play with marked cards, to toy with superstition when he was a philosopher and natural scientist whose function was to fight against ignorance – these things inevitably wounded his finer feelings. But he could not allow himself to be destroyed just because he had finer feelings. He could not go into debt to the tune of fifteen hundred daler (as the sum had finally become), which he would never be able to pay off. Why should he lose his honour and reduce his family to penury? No, he would not go under: his desire to live and his belief in his greater right to life made him rise in arms against his imminent enslavement to a barbarian who through idleness and drink would consume whatever he – a man of learning – earned. No, he would be the hangman who placed the hood over the barbarian's head. The time had come to draw a line under centuries of culture and his own acquired concepts of honour and conscience: better to sacrifice the peace of his soul, to surrender some of the self-respect which made life tolerable for him. He would have to bear the burden of his secret, for he knew that the murder might haunt him just as fear of life after death haunted his enemy. Did this fear of striking the lethal blow reveal a weakness in the constitution of his soul, just as the fear of dying revealed a weakness in his enemy? Did these weaknesses spring from the same source? He refused to admit to such a possibility for, when he compared himself with the gipsy, he was certain that the vital elements of his soul were more fitted to the purposes of present society than those of the pariah. The pariah, whether he was a migrant from Egypt or the Far East or whether he was merely the lowest stratum of the half-savage people of southern Europe, had retained all those base instincts inimical to social order. He and his kind are incapable of work. They cannot settle and found a nation or a family and so they have been perpetual nomads, moving from country to country in search of loot and plunder: which is why the laws of the nations treat them as thieves and subject them to legislation under which they stand with one foot outside the common law. It was this anarchic way of life, with no thought of the morrow and no desire for settled property and national allegiance, that nourished the gipsy's fear of the future. The future can offer no security to those who merely live for today: herein lay the source of his insecurity and of his fear of people – from whom he can expect nothing because he has nothing to give in return; and herein lay his fear of death – of which he knows nothing, does not wish to know anything and does not dare to hear anything.

What, then, lay at the heart of Törner's disquiet about crushing this opponent? It was his sense of the value of human life, the doctrine that we should forgive our enemies, defeated or not. Old and foolish teachings which malevolent men have always availed themselves of to overthrow those who have been merciful in victory; stories of the blessings of compassion – omitting, of course, the story of the frozen serpent which turned on the breast that warmed it. All those pretty teachings about the value of the individual, about self-respect and about God, who alone has the right to vengeance. Törner had already rejected many of these archaic doctrines but at this moment, just as he was about to put his new understanding of the relative nature of human value into practice, something caused his hand to hesitate half way to the heart of his enemy: his searching and doubting spirit was held back by the doctrine that the common people are sacred whereas those who govern them are not.

So he was doomed simply because he was a civilized man, one who has evolved to a higher social plane and is thus destined to see himself brought down by the same fate that struck down the civilized nations of the past: defeated by barbarians because they could not murder like barbarians, steal like barbarians, betray like barbarians. The fruits of enlightenment, of morality and of justice were that the enlightened, moral and learned man could not defend himself because he lacked the requisite brutality!

All this philosophizing distracted Törner's mind from what lay ahead and he had to remind himself of the mockery, the coarseness, the infamy he had been subjected to. As he did this, focusing utterly on the single hard nub that held his oldest and strongest instincts, he felt enormous power flowing into him as he repeated time after time: he is a tyrant and he will enslave his fellow men! Kill him!

Tyrant! That was the word his more profound philosophizing had failed to produce. He understood perfectly well that the concepts tyrant and ruler, tyrant and dictator, tyrant and overlord, could easily coincide, and this single word was sufficient to remind him of nature's great hatred of oppression. It wakened the ancient slave instincts in him, revived the passions of the savage, allowed him to don the cloak of barbarian thought and action. He emerged so to speak from his own personality and, finding himself subject to the base creature whose heel was on his neck, hated him with all the hatred of the subjugated. He imagined that his opponent was the ruler and he a child of the common people who, year in and year out, was forced to slave and toil for the idle scum, give him his blood and his soul as his forefathers had done. And now at last he rose up, savage and filled with rage, and grasped his cudgel to kill his foe, to crush his skull and cast his corpse to the dogs.

But he turned back yet again, laid down his cudgel and sat at the table.

No, open warfare was not the way. He had fought in the wars himself, firing on his enemies with no second thoughts. He had defended himself with his cudgel in the classroom, breaking arms and legs with no feelings other than the pain from the blows he received in return. That was war but this was murder. Ah, but tyrants refuse to be drawn into open battle, so they must be murdered! And this tyrant must die.

*

Fear and terror – those were the means of destroying the already frightened gipsy! Törner knew that to achieve this he would need to make the shades of the dead gatekeeper and his wife *come back and haunt* the gipsy. Whether this would be enough, only time would tell. He must be prepared for everything, he must drive in the knife wherever there was bare flesh and cut him to ribbons.

In a state of excitement he recollected the gipsy telling him of a recurrent dream in which he was first transformed into a grass snake, then into a rat and finally into a dog, at which point he always woke in great anxiety. Törner did not believe in dreams as prophecies of the future but he did attribute to them some significance, as yet unresearched, as memories that possibly emanated from our pre-existence among our ancestors. Why did this dream repeatedly return to the gipsy and fill him with terror?

Could it be the result of distant memories from primeval times when his forefathers believed – like the Egyptians – in metempsychosis or the transmigration of the soul into animals after death? And why did this particular dream terrify him? Perhaps it was because our life force has such a consistent and inherent urge to develop towards higher forms that the mere thought of returning to a lower level struck terror into the heart of a man like the gipsy, so hungry to rise in the world. Törner recollected that the worst recurring dreams he himself suffered revolved around being a child at school. The idea of retreating in time and age had a crippling impact on him and he would lose all his self-confidence for the whole day after such a dream: he felt that his children were as old as he was and that he himself had shrunk.

He knew that, somehow, on the basis of these vague suppositions, he had to come up with a solution but what that solution might be he did not know. Given the erratic workings of the gipsy's mind it was impossible to proceed systematically. But Törner was sure that, if he could stage a performance that surpassed the gipsy's dream in terms of tangible reality, it would prove utterly overpowering, crushing and suffocating in its effect. All the more so if he reinforced it with the apparitions of the dead he was now painting.

So he painted his pictures big and bold so the gipsy would be able to recognize them without difficulty, and he set up his magic lantern. For the pictures to work without the lantern being visible the light had to come from behind the observer, but Törner had to be prepared for the possibility of his victim turning round to investigate the source of the images. In order to obviate the need to extinguish or screen the lantern he constructed a triangle of three tubes filled with phosphorus and fixed them round the lantern to make it resemble the all-seeing eye above the altar in a church. The gipsy had a choice: he could interpret it either as being the blinding eye of God or as the eye that had been carved on the tree.

*

Everything was ready and Törner was waiting for the right moment. A day passed and the second was coming to its end.

The gipsy had taken to addressing him in intrusively familiar terms, had 'borrowed' a number of his books, tobacco and supplies of drink and had been lying all day on the roof of the privy – from where he could observe Törner's window – drinking and smoking.

He was expecting to receive his loan the following morning and had therefore been watching with great interest for the arrival of the post-rider who would bring the money Törner had promised.

Not having received any wages the week before, all the workers had left and the sequestration of the estate was expected at any moment. An uncanny stillness hung over the deserted estate, where the starving dogs, now scarcely able to move, lay in wait for rats, sparrows or dung-beetles to still their hunger.

The cattle had been slaughtered and eaten and only the horses remained. They stood leaning against the bare fruit-trees in the garden as if waiting to go to their eternal rest. The hens went about under the cherry-tree pecking at cherry-stones the magpies had already spat out.

The tumbledown house resembled a sinking ship. But the

peacock still stood on the great dung-heap and spread his magnificent tail, by now a little frayed and dull after a summer of not being fed, but still fine and beautiful. Amidst the filth he was all there was to please the eye.

Törner had invited the gipsy to supper so as to avoid an invitation from him: to be forced to endure rotting food, awful drinks and dirty service would have been an additional torment. But he had another purpose in mind for this final meeting. He needed to prepare his victim for some hours to make him receptive to the process that was to follow.

Wearing his official dress, with a sword at his side and claiming to have been visiting the priest, Törner went down to the summerhouse where the gipsy was waiting for him. His unusually formal attire did not fail to make the intended impression and, from force of habit, the gipsy raised his hat, did not dare address him in familiar terms but made various servile gestures and adopted his most urbane manner. The table was set with a shining white damask cloth and gleaming plates and glasses, and there were both knives and forks, which caused the gipsy considerable embarrassment.

There were to be few courses but they were well-prepared and the wine, a vintage Syracuse, gleamed golden-yellow in a silver jug, gilt on the inside.

Everything was arranged to impress and Törner's earnest, measured but courteous deportment had an immediate impact on the gipsy, who quickly realized that he would need to behave with propriety.

Törner carved the meat and served his guest, who repeatedly asked him not to go to any trouble on his behalf even though Törner's stiff manner demonstrated clearly enough that it was for his own sake, from a sense of duty to himself and his rank, that he was observing the customs of good society.

Once they had eaten and the glasses were filled Master Andreas Törner began to speak. He began by touching on various topics that might catch the gipsy's attention without encouraging him to respond. He revealed some of the secrets of the life of plants and animals, discoursing in particular on the wonders of the animal world, while the gipsy listened respectfully. But every time the gipsy attempted to butt in with his own opinions, Törner showed such obvious impatience that it was clear he was only waiting for the gipsy to finish his inane remarks so that he could continue without either answering or referring to the interruptions. As time passed even the gipsy tired of trying and sat there as a silent listener.

Having captured the gipsy's attention he switched to other topics, moving quickly in the direction he intended: theology and the mysteries of life and death. He posited philosophical explanations of the most profound kind so that the gipsy, no longer having anything to interpose, struggled to remain attentive – a difficult task for a savage or a child. His face went pale with exhaustion and his eyes grew small.

As he talked Törner encouraged his guest to drink, not with the intention of getting him drunk but to let the fiery wine ignite his imagination.

The gipsy seemed close to losing consciousness and stood up at intervals to avoid looking into the fiery eyes that were mesmerizing him, burning into his brain and holding him in a vice. But Törner immediately took hold of him again. No sooner did the gipsy try to say something than he lost all desire to do so since Törner would immediately look away or look down as if preoccupied. This continued for three hours until at last the gipsy tried to break free and end the conversation by asking permission to sing a song.

Master Törner said it would be a pleasure but, when the gipsy saw the dull and vacant expression on his listener's face, his will to continue faded and the song died away in the second verse.

Darkness had fallen now and the lamps were lit. The evening was overcast and a gentle breeze soughed through the rushes on the lake.

The gipsy's mind was excited by wine and exertion and a host of fantasies were struggling to reach the surface. So many seeds had been sown that they were bursting the cortex of his brain, just as the parasitic mistletoe splits the bark of its host tree. His thoughts were in ferment. He had been presented with the whole of theology and cosmogony; the most profound questions had flashed past him, awakening his curiosity and the desire to ask a thousand questions in return; his old ideas had been turned upside down; his stock of ready-made opinions about life and death, existence and pre-existence had been upset; above all, confusion and disorder reigned in his mind which, although fertile, was incapable of producing anything but barren seed since he lacked all scientific knowledge.

When, after five hours, Törner considered he had weakened his will sufficiently for him to be ready to follow every one of his exorcist's commands, he finally released him. But, with his stronger spirit and will, Törner continued to control the gipsy's thoughts and, as night approached with the darkness deepening and the wind whining eerily, he began to tell stories of ghosts. He told of white ladies, of spectres and phantoms, until the gipsy sat there shaken to the core waiting for the moment he was permitted to tell of the apparitions *he* had seen.

At last Törner allowed the gipsy to speak and spurred his imagination by following him with utter concentration, staring at his victim, offering him a receptive sounding-board, encouraging him to continue and luring him out into the dangerous waters of fabrication by pretending to believe everything while exaggerating his own gullibility and sympathy.

The gipsy now gave free rein to his overblown imagination, exciting himself to the point where, time after time, he looked at the bushes, fearful of seeing something there, and then glancing furtively at Törner's sword to reassure himself.

Master Törner responded by recounting the most horrifying stories he could recall and finally, when the gipsy was in the throes of excitement, he rose, apologized for breaking up the party and said goodnight.

'I think I'm going to be afraid of the dark tonight,' the gipsy said in an attempt at flippancy.

'Well, for my part, I think I'd rather sleep outside,' Törner answered without really knowing what he meant by it.

'Outside?'

'Yes. Because there are no ghosts outside – not if you light a fire, anyway.'

Afterwards he found it impossible to explain why he had mentioned fire but it may have been that he vaguely remembered that negroes sleep with lighted fires to scare away wild animals.

Once he had coaxed the gipsy away from the summerhouse he called the maid, asked her to light the candles in his turret room and then he slipped back to the summerhouse unobserved and took his magic lantern from its basket.

Without really knowing what would happen next or how best to proceed, Törner lit his pipe. He was weary beyond belief and the payment of the promised loan the next day threatened to end his life and his hopes.

Meanwhile the maid returned, cleared the table, took away the plates and bowls and, when she had finished, asked him to douse the lights himself.

This reminded him that he was sitting in the light whereas he needed darkness. When the girl had gone he extinguished the candles.

A gentle breeze rustled across the fields bringing with it a dense, damp mist which hung and thickened over the woods. Törner suddenly leapt to his feet for he saw something gleaming in the mist out across the meadow and realized that the gipsy had lighted a peat fire. Carrying his lantern Törner crept to an empty shed from which he could look over the meadow without being seen.

He saw the gipsy lying out there by a smoking fire, his back turned to the shed. He was wrapped in a woollen blanket that had once been white but now only showed up slightly lighter than the surrounding darkness. On the far side of the fire the smoke and mist hung over the edge of the woods and formed a wall as solid as any Törner could have wished for.

He lit his lantern and the figure of a woman dressed in black and wearing a white veil immediately emerged from the peat smoke.

At first the gipsy seemed unaware of it but when the figure moved, stirred by the next puff of wind, he leapt to his feet and stared into the fire.

To prevent him examining the image too closely, Törner made the figure disappear and then reappear in the smoke, and each time he slid the glass plate in and out of the lantern the gipsy jumped, leapt up and fell down.

It was as if Törner had the gipsy on a string and could set him in motion with a twitch of his finger.

Now, having caught the gipsy's attention, he projected an enormous image of the gatekeeper on the wall of mist and smoke.

It was a terrifying sight: a gigantic shrouded corpse appeared to be approaching from the woods with its hand raised and even Törner felt the dreadful eeriness of the vision. By twisting the lens he made the image come closer and closer and he heard the gipsy begin to howl softly, a continuous, monotonous howl as from a madman; and he saw him draw the blanket over his head, stand up, dance like a bear, fall down on the grass and rise again until he stood there paralysed, like a man with lockjaw, howling gently and incessantly.

Then the gatekeeper disappeared and the first act of the drama was over.

But the gipsy remained standing utterly motionless like a statue, while from the smoke a grass-snake crawled, as if alive, with its yellow ears and pointed forked tongue.

The image was so clear and the colours so lifelike that the gipsy could not fail to see it.

And he saw it. As it slithered through the restlessly billowing smoke the gipsy's paralysis slowly left him, his body began to move in time with the movements of the snake and he began to twist his shoulders and back like a swimmer sliding through the water.

Fearing that exhaustion would break the spell, Törner slid a new plate into the lantern and projected the grass-snake metamorphosing into a rat on the densest area of smoke.

The gipsy sank slowly to the ground, drew his legs up under

him and, with squeaking noises, began to sniff at all the molehills while now and then looking up at the smoky image that seemed to have trapped him in an invisible web.

The gipsy's brain was now locked into a fixed path and the road it would follow was predetermined. Even before the next image was revealed, he had raised himself up on all fours with his blanket still wrapped around him and, as the form of a hound emerged from the smoke, he began baying horrifically as if this was the moment he had been waiting for. Then a fearful noise came from the back steps of the house and the back door slammed open and shut eight times as the eight starving hounds charged out to attack the unknown intruder.

At that moment Master Törner knew what the end would be and, to hasten it, he pointed the lantern down so that the image of the hound shone directly on the white blanket.

The pack did not hesitate: all eight joined in a raging, howling mass that pounced on their master and tore him to death.

*

The pariah was dead, the Aryan victorious. Victorious thanks to his knowledge and spiritual superiority to the inferior race. But had he not found the strength to commit a crime he could easily have been the victim.

Now that his enemy was defeated he could look on him with forgiveness; and later, when he sat in the university library reading the laws of the sage Manu,* he understood the hate that had been directed at him, understood the whole chain of vile deeds perpetrated by a man to whom he had done nothing but good, to whom he had offered his hand, but who had arrogantly struck him down and laughed at his expense. He understood now the love of

---

* The Law Book of Manu is the best known of the collections of classical Indian law. The stipulations as to how Tschandala, the lowest Indian caste, is to be treated may be found in verse 51ff. of the tenth book of Manu's Law Book. [Author's note]

filth and crime, the predilection for all kinds of putrefaction, the sympathy for unclean animals.

These are the words the wise Manu wrote with the aim of creating – by a process of humiliation – a race of the humiliated, destined to occupy the lowest level of all and form the warm nourishing dung from which the noble Aryan stock would be able to shoot and flower every hundred years like the aloe:

Tschandala, the fruit of adultery, incest and crime, may only eat garlic and bulbs that taste of putrefaction; and no-one may bring him corn and fruits or water and fire.

Tschandala may not draw water from rivers, springs or wells but only from fens and the puddles that gather in the tracks of cattle.

Tschandala may not wash, for water is only granted him to quench his thirst.

Tschandala may never own a fixed abode; may only dress in clothes taken from corpses; may only eat from damaged utensils, wear scrap iron as jewels and worship evil spirits.

Thus wrote the sage Manu.

HJALMAR BERGMAN

Memoirs of a Dead Man

(translated by Neil Smith)

'Not everyone who lives is alive; nor is death a portal that only opens in one direction'

Hjalmar Bergman (1883-1931) is widely regarded as one of the foremost Swedish novelists of the twentieth century. *Memoirs of a Dead Man*, first published in 1918, follows the efforts of Jan Arnberg, the 'dead man' of the title (although there are numerous other candidates worthy of the description among Bergman's gallery of characters), to escape the curse that has bound the fate of his family to that of the Arnfelts for generations.

The earlier efforts of Jan's father to break free of the curse by moving to America founder in a biting parody of consumer society and advertising slogans. Jan's own story culminates when he has to flee a small-town scandal in Sweden and ends up in a symbolic kingdom of death in Hamburg, a mixture of casino and high-class brothel, where the family curse is played out once more, and where he comes to realize that abdication from free will is his only option.

Although apparently realistic to begin with, Bergman's novel shifts towards a theatrical, dreamlike world of repetitions and refractions in which the fates of his characters are predetermined and acted out in a macabre mixture of comedy and nightmare. Characters presumed dead manifest themselves in incidental roles throughout the novel, casting a foreboding light on the almost biblical nature of the family curse.

ISBN 978 1 870041 65 2
UK £10.95
(paperback, 352 pages)

HJALMAR SÖDERBERG

Martin Birck's Youth

(translated by Tom Ellett)

Hjalmar Söderberg's partly autobiographical second novel was originally published in 1901, and traces the development of the title character from a seemingly idyllic Stockholm childhood to maturity as a thirty-year-old man, an introspective outsider, critical of society, constantly searching for the truth but going through a gradual process of disillusionment. He dreams of being a poet, but is too melancholic to break free from his modest bureaucratic career, and slowly drifts towards nihilism and aestheticism.

Martin Birck's Youth is a book rich in fin-de-siècle themes: melancholy, eroticism and decadence abound. The Stockholm depicted here is a haunting city of shadows and snowstorms, suppressed passion and loneliness. The conflict between dreams and reality which occurs in so many novels of the period is central to the novel, and its preoccupation with issues of free will, determinism and morality prefigures Söderberg's next novel, the highly acclaimed *Doctor Glas* (in which Martin Birch makes a cameo appearance).

ISBN 978 1 870041 59 3
UK £8.95
(paperback, 152 pages)

RUNAR SCHILDT

The Meat-Grinder
and Other Stories

(translated by Martin and Anna-Lisa Murrell)

Runar Schildt (1888-1925) is one of the major figures of Finland-Swedish literature, and one of Finland's finest short-story writers. His precisely observed depictions of Helsingfors life in the early decades of the twentieth century, his acute sense of irony and delicately drawn characters place him firmly among the foremost exponents of the European short story.

This anthology brings together stories from different stages of Schildt's career for the first time in English. His early writing depicts the decadence and heady social whirl of upper-class Helsingfors in the years preceding the Finnish Civil War of 1918. 'The Weaker One', regarded by many to be Schildt's masterpiece, is a particularly sharply drawn story of adultery and deception.

ISBN 978 1 870041 56 0
UK £9.95
(paperback, 318 pages)

For further information, or to request a catalogue, contact:
Norvik Press, University of East Anglia (LLT), Norwich NR4 7TJ, England
e-mail: norvik.press@uea.ac.uk

Website: www.norvikpess.com